"I'm going to kiss
you good night, firefly,"
the soft voice warned.

"You are not!" she protested fiercely, trying to draw back.

"I've been kissing my dates good night since I was fourteen," Jason stated matter-of-factly. "I'm not about to stop now."

"I am *not* your date, Jason Carlysle—never have been and never will be. Would you please let me go?"

"In a minute. I want to be sure of something first." His hands continued to hold her, and she was waiting breathlessly for something to happen; but his gently curving lips kept their distance while his long fingers continued to play their tantalizing dance over her face. She couldn't control the wild fandango of her pulses, the liquid sensation in her lower body...

Dear Reader:

Spring is just around the corner! And we've got six new SECOND CHANCE AT LOVE romances to keep you cozy until it arrives. So sit back, put your feet up, and enjoy . . .

You've also got a lot to look forward to in the months ahead—delightful romances from exciting new writers, as well as fabulous stories from your tried-and-true favorites. You know you can rely on SECOND CHANCE AT LOVE to provide the kind of satisfying romantic entertainment you expect.

We continue to receive and enjoy your letters—so please keep them coming! Remember: Your thoughts and feelings about SECOND CHANCE AT LOVE books are what enable us to publish the kind of romances you not only enjoy reading once, but also keep in a special place and read again and again.

Warm wishes for a beautiful spring,

Ellen Edwards

Ellen Edwards
SECOND CHANCE AT LOVE
The Berkley Publishing Group
200 Madison Avenue
New York, N.Y. 10016

Second Chance at Love®

IRRESISTIBLE YOU

CLAUDIA BISHOP

**A SECOND CHANCE AT LOVE
BOOK**

For Kate

Requests for permission to make copies of any part of the work should be mailed to: Permissions, Second Chance at Love, The Berkley Publishing Group, 200 Madison Avenue, New York, NY 10016.

First edition published April 1984

First printing

"Second Chance at Love" and the butterfly emblem are trademarks belonging to Jove Publications, Inc.

Printed in the United States of America

Second Chance at Love books are published by
The Berkley Publishing Group
200 Madison Avenue, New York, NY 10016

Chapter 1

NOTHING HAD GONE according to plan today, and now she'd missed the six o'clock shuttle! The seven o'clock would never get her home in time for that meeting, thought Vanessa Harrington as she hurled herself across the madhouse that was La Guardia Airport at the height of the evening commuter rush. She'd have to try for a regular flight, and that meant changing terminals.

As she reached the desk, something happened to the ground beneath her feet—it began to slide very fast, upward and away from her. She dropped everything and grabbed wildly, desperately, for the nearest available solid object. The object turned out to be a navy-suited forearm instantly hardening into a steely support under her grasping fingers.

"Oh, I'm so sorry," she gasped. "I don't know what happened. There must be something sticky on the floor." She raised her head and found herself looking into the most humorous pair of gray eyes she had ever encountered.

"Your arrival was certainly a bit precipitate," the stranger said, laughing. "Are you quite stable now?"

"Yes...yes, thank you," she stammered, trying for a smile, wondering suddenly and quite uncharacteristically what she looked like at this moment. She could feel her red-gold hair escaping from its usual neat topknot, and her cheeks were hot. Was she perspiring, too?

"You seem to have created a degree of chaos," the rich

voice went on, soft laughter in its depths. "Perhaps we should pick up the papers you dropped."

Vanessa looked horror-struck at the sea of scattered papers surrounding her feet, some of the neatly typed pages already bearing grubby footprints from heedless passersby. "I can't afford to lose any of this!" she exclaimed, dropping to her knees instantly and gathering up the fruits of two months' work.

"This is probably an impertinent comment, but isn't it inviting trouble to carry around loose papers in a manila folder? Briefcases do exist." He was on his knees beside her, still laughing as he piled up a stack of sheets and handed them over.

"Yes, I know." She took the pages, inserting them hastily into the inadequate folder. "It's just that the handle on mine broke this morning as I was leaving home." She sat back on her heels, trying to tuck the unruly strands of her hair back into the loose pins.

"Please, allow me." Before she could protest, a pair of square, competent hands were swiftly tidying up her hair. Long, sensitive fingers moved across her scalp with a disturbingly intimate touch.

"Thank you," Vanessa muttered, feeling very peculiar under the scrutiny of those amused gray eyes.

"Hold on a minute—we missed one." He twisted to one side suddenly, picking up the lone diagram and examining it with a frown. "What's this?"

"It's a flow chart," she replied promptly.

"Well, yes, I can see that. But it's a very unusual one." He handed it back to her.

"It's a motivation-flow," she said enthusiastically. "You see—"

"Hey, hold on a second." An imperative palm lifted. "I am utterly fascinated, but I have a plane to catch and I assume you do, too."

She grinned ruefully. "I just missed the six o'clock shuttle to Washington. I was hoping to catch the next regular flight—hence the hundred-yard dash."

"In that case, Vanessa Harrington, we'd better get a move

on. You can tell me all about motivation-flows when we're in the air." He stood up in one easy movement and extended a hand.

"How do you know my name?" Frowning, she put her own hand in his and allowed him to pull her to her feet. The firm clasp sent prickly tingles up her arm.

"I've just been picking up your papers, remember?" came the smooth explanation. "I have very sharp eyes."

Not just sharp, either, Vanessa thought distractedly, turning to the woman behind the desk who'd been watching their antics with considerable interest.

"You're going to Washington, too, then?" The inquiry was as neutral as she could manage. She handed over her credit card, waiting for the woman to process it.

"I was certainly intending to," the rich voice agreed, "but if I hadn't been, I'd be changing my plans right now. It's not every day that a firefly lands on my arm."

Help! Vanessa cried silently. Things were getting out of hand around here. She took her boarding card with a polite, abstracted smile of thanks and turned away from the desk.

Her chance-met companion was waiting, leaning easily against the desk, his slim briefcase standing between black, beautifully shined shoes. Vanessa had never thought of herself as particularly small before—just an average five feet five—but the top of her head was level with a very broad shoulder, and her eyes met only an expanse of a silky pale-blue shirt, the neat knot of a burgundy-colored tie. With an effort, she raised her eyes to meet a smile that sent shock waves to the soles of her feet.

"You'll have to run," the woman behind the desk said briskly. "They're about to close the gate."

"Come along then, Miss—or is it Mrs.?—Harrington. And hang on to those papers!" Her hand was seized again and she had to run to keep up with her companion's long stride. Not for the first time, Vanessa blessed her preference for sensible shoes—they might not be the most elegant footwear, but at least they made running feasible.

Her hair was bouncing out of its chignon again as they reached the gate. Their hand baggage went through the scanner, with Vanessa reluctantly consigning the precious folder of loose papers to the moving belt.

"I think you need a new briefcase pretty quickly," her companion said, grinning at her.

"So do I," she murmured, gathering everything up at the other end of the conveyor and clutching the folder to her chest with a relieved sigh.

They walked down the rubber-coated ramp, under the grooved canopy, and into the crowded airplane.

"Over here!" Her shoulder was gripped firmly but lightly. She obeyed the gently insistent pressure as the tall stranger piloted her down the aisle and into one of two vacant seats side by side in the middle section.

"So, which is it?" The man beside her fastened his seat belt with swift, practiced movements.

"Which is what?" Vanessa queried.

"Miss or Mrs.?" He laughed.

"Doctor, actually," she replied evasively.

"Ahhh." Silence fell as the plane began to move slowly. They reached the beginning of the runway and Vanessa felt her body slip into a familiar relaxation; she was in someone else's hands for the next fifty minutes. The engines roared and she rested against the high, straight seat back, eyes half-closed. The airplane gathered speed along the tarmac until, effortlessly, it took to the air. Finally, it leveled off and the flight attendant's bright voice declared: "The captain has turned off the no smoking sign, but for your comfort and convenience we ask that you keep your seat belts fastened for the duration of . . ."

"Doctor of what?" The question brought her out of her reverie. "I'll lay odds you're not a medical doctor—they don't prepare motivation-flows."

"Why so interested?" she asked lightly.

"As I said: It's not every day a firefly lands on my arm." He turned sideways in his seat; her heart did a wild flip-flop under that soft, gray-eyed, laughing look.

"Let me buy you a drink? I owe you, I think," she said swiftly as the flight attendant approached with the beverage cart.

"Scotch and water, then," he drawled. "Thank you."

Vanessa bought herself a gin and tonic as well as a miniature bottle of Scotch for her companion.

"If you really don't want to answer my question, that's your business, of course. But you might just say so, instead of this studious avoidance." The face holding hers carried no laughter now, just a quiet puzzlement.

"Which question?" she asked, wondering why on earth she was being so evasive. The man was only making conversation, after all.

"I asked two. Why don't you choose which one you'd like to answer first." He took the plastic glass in front of him, raised it to his lips. He sipped slowly, reflectively.

"I have a doctorate in clinical psychology, and my specialization is personnel problems in a corporate setting," she informed him.

"So, *Dr.* Harrington, what do you do to earn your living in this tough world of ours?"

"I run my own business," Vanessa said succinctly.

The figure beside her sighed heavily. "As answers go, that was among the least informative I've ever received."

Vanessa took a quick sip of her drink, pushing the ice cubes around with the plastic swizzle stick. "I'm an industrial consultant," she said eventually. "I work in a fairly new field. Companies are beginning to realize that there are ways to deal with unproductive employees other than firing them or deciding to live with their mistakes because they're almost at retirement age."

"Well, go on," prodded the quiet voice of her companion. "I assume this is where motivation-flow charts come in?"

"Exactly!" This was familiar, exciting territory, and Vanessa needed no further prompting. "I get called in when management decides to beef up production and performance. The companies that use my services tend to be fairly progressive, willing to look within their own structure to find answers and remedies to personnel problems. I work on the principle that everyone actually *wants* to work at full potential—they just need the right motivation and the right environment to do so."

"You mean there's no such thing as the individual out for a quick, easy buck?" The voice beside her was no longer amused but frankly skeptical.

"Oh, there are a few, of course. But most poor performance has its roots in managerial inefficiency," Vanessa responded blithely.

"I'm sorry to disagree, Dr. Harrington, but I have a small problem with your philosophy. People work because they need to, not because they want to. They have to put bread on the table, pay the bills, worry about putting their kids through college."

"That's just the sort of attitude that produces underachievers," she said swiftly. "You have to start from the premise that everyone *could* be interested in their job, from the lowliest warehouse employee to the president." She shot him a quick look, surprising an expression of startled interest on the lean face.

"How did you get into this field, Dr. Harrington?"

She smiled. "My undergraduate major was psychology and I went for my doctorate full of ideals—no private practice at the end for me! I planned to work at an inner-city clinic that offered clients low-cost psychotherapy." She gave a slightly self-conscious shrug. She had always found it rather embarrassing to talk about what so many people found hard to understand—what her former husband, Gideon, during their quarrels, had always referred to as her "wishy-washy liberalism."

"So what happened to the ideals?" the voice prompted gently.

"Oh, they haven't disappeared, just got redirected," she explained. "I spent a summer working in a factory—screwing tops on bottles. Dante's Inferno couldn't have been worse. The incessant noise, the heat, the mindlessness of it all!" A shudder rippled her slim shoulders. "Everything was made worse by the petty power politics of a rigid hierarchy. You couldn't even get off the line to go to the bathroom without raising your hand like a first-grader. And some of the line supervisors had a remarkable capacity for selective blindness!"

She took a quick sip of her drink, wondering why it was so easy to talk to this calm stranger. "Anyway, it occurred to me that my . . . talents, if you like, could be directed toward improving the day-to-day lot of a larger number of people than those who find their way to mental-health clinics."

Her companion nodded. "But didn't that mean changing your course of studies?"

She grinned reminiscently. "It certainly did. I changed my thesis subject, midyear, to an examination of stress management—or rather, the lack of it—on the shop floor. Fortunately, I had a very understanding supervisor. He suggested that I go on to do an MBA—on the principle that I could be more effective if I were familiar with both sides of the coin."

Her companion quirked a thoughtful eyebrow. "But aren't you now working completely on the management side? They're the ones buying your services, after all."

"True, but my primary emphasis is on bettering the lot of the employee. Still, I don't disillusion the management if they like to think I'm working for them." Her neighbor chuckled appreciatively. "If my efforts are successful, then both sides benefit. Of course, in many cases problems lie outside the company, in the employees' personal lives. Part of my job is to set up an employee-assistance program that allows these problems to be discussed confidentially with a professional therapist, and also provides referrals to outside organizations."

She looked sideways at her companion. He was lying back in his tilted chair, long legs stretched outward into the aisle. The picture of relaxation—or was he? There was something about that tall, sinewy body that shouted control, and she remembered the way his arm had instantly responded to her clutching fingers.

As if in response to her scrutiny, he turned his head toward her and her heart did its crazy flip-flop again. He wasn't conventionally handsome, but his lean, craggy face was compellingly attractive, with deep-set eyes that were now narrowed slightly, a wide brow furrowed in thought, a full mouth set in a firm line. A long-fingered hand ran reflectively over a very determined jawline and strong chin.

"So you run a rescue service for poor exploited workers, do you? Starting from the principle that poor performance, numerous sick days, and excessively long lunch hours are in general the fault of the employer—right?"

"Wrong! That's not what I said," Vanessa protested hotly. "The fact that the working environment may need improving isn't synonymous with an exploitative employer—"

"All right, firefly, calm down," the deep voice interrupted her. "Sorry if I pushed the wrong button there." He laughed at her indignant expression. "Let's do something about that flyaway red hair of yours. It seems to be somewhat affected by your enthusiasm."

His hands were on her head a second time, deftly twisting the loose tendrils into the pins. "I don't know why you don't just let it down," he suggested, laughing softly. "It clearly doesn't like being confined in this ridiculous knot!"

"It was fine this morning," she insisted, wondering why she was explaining anything to this disconcertingly intimate stranger. "I've been rushing around all day."

"Yes, I had noticed," he replied gravely.

Vanessa choked on her drink. A firm hand patted her back between her shoulder blades.

"Well, at least I've got a laugh out of you," the man went on. "I was beginning to think you were so occupied with the world's problems that you couldn't find anything funny."

"You know nothing about me," Vanessa announced, sitting up straight in her chair as she decided abruptly that this conversation had gone on quite long enough. "Well, perhaps that's not entirely true," she amended. "You know certain facts about me. The only thing I know about you is that you have very quick reflexes." And the most engaging, crinkly eyes and the widest, most generous mouth, she added silently.

"I tell you what, Vanessa Harrington—how about you answer my first question and then I'll answer one of yours." There was a serious look on the intelligent face now, as if for some reason her answer might be important.

"You mean, am I Miss or Mrs.?" she asked.

"You know damn well that's what I mean!" he said in exasperation. "Now, are you married or aren't you?"

"Not right now," Vanessa said swiftly.

He laughed then, his whole body radiating enjoyment. "What on earth does that mean? Are you saying you were yesterday, might be again tomorrow, but today you decided not to be?"

Her own soft peal of laughter joined his. "What an absurd way of putting it. I'm sorry! I have been married, I'm not now, and don't have any intentions of becoming so ever again. And that's all the information you're getting. It's my turn now."

"Very well, one question, then."

"That's not fair," she protested. "You asked me dozens."

"No, I didn't. Only six, actually, and five of those were connected." He grinned disarmingly.

"Well, you have a name, presumably?" she said.

"Yes, I do," was the prompt reply.

"Oh, who's being absurd now?" She chuckled.

"I was just giving you a taste of your own medicine," he said blandly, but his eyes were gleaming again.

"All right, I've swallowed it and didn't enjoy the taste! Now, your name . . . ?"

"Jason." He smiled devilishly.

"Jason what?" Vanessa groaned.

"Ah, now that, firefly, you're going to have to wait to find out," he murmured. "We need to keep *some* mystery for the next time."

The deep voice carried such promise that Vanessa felt her palms moisten. The image of Gideon rose with uncomfortable vividness in her mind's eye and she bit her bottom lip hard, forcing herself back to reality. It was a dangerous line of thought—remembering that wonderful, fluttery sensation her ex-husband had always managed to create, and that was now being created by a near stranger!

"You're assuming we're going to be taking the same plane again, are you?" she said lightly.

"That's always possible, of course," was the smooth response. "But I prefer not to leave things to chance if I can help it."

The slight bump as the plane touched down, and the violent roar of the engines in reverse thrust as they came to a halt, saved Vanessa from the need to reply—fortunately, she reflected, since she had no idea how to respond. Further conversation was impossible in the scramble for the terminal.

"Can I drop you anywhere?" her companion asked as they stood, an island of intense quiet in the sea of hurrying, frenetic travelers around them.

She shook her head. "No, thank you, my car's in the lot. I have to go straight to a meeting in Old Town, Alexandria." Now why had she volunteered that piece of information?

"You work a long day, Dr. Harrington," he stated matter-of-factly.

"On occasion," she agreed simply.

"Well, thank you for making my flight so enjoyable." He smiled down at her and she swallowed convulsively, her body heating under the gently humorous appraisal.

"Thank *you*."

"Until the next time, then." With a slight mock bow, he turned and made his way to the exit.

"Oh, Lord," Vanessa breathed, watching the broad, blue-suited back maneuver easily through the crowds, noticing absently how the brown hair curled in graying tendrils at the nape of his neck.

It was nearly midnight when she wearily let herself into her riverside condominium.

"Did you get the contract?" a sleepy voice called from the living room.

"You still up, Jilly? Yes I did." She entered the softly lit room and smiled cheerfully at her roommate, who was sitting propped on the couch surrounded by heavy tomes. Jilly grinned, giving her small face under its sleek cap of short fair hair the look of a mischievous pixie. Her bright-blue eyes sparkled, belying her obvious fatigue.

"Lord, what are you doing?" Vanessa questioned, indicating the volumes. "Lawyers aren't supposed to work into the early hours." She shot her friend a concerned glance. "You look exhausted, Jilly!"

"I'm summing up in the Parker case tomorrow," her roommate replied. "I was looking for a precedent—without much success, I'm afraid. Have you eaten? I left some soup on the stove."

"No thanks." Vanessa sighed. "I'm too tired for hunger, but I'm going to have a nightcap. Want one?"

"Sure." Jilly got off the couch and stretched her diminutive body wearily, pressing her hands into the small of her back to ease the stiffness. "Oh, by the way, Gideon has called three times tonight."

"Thoroughly disturbing your concentration, I suppose." Vanessa smiled apologetically, handing her friend a glass. "He seems to think that because you and I have known each other since we were eleven he can harass you as much as he does me. Did he say what he wanted?"

"Something about the Hatteras house."

"I wish he'd agree to sell that damn place." Vanessa sipped her brandy. "I don't need a piece of jointly owned property to keep reminding me of our now dead partnership."

"You have the right to insist that he sell it, Van."

"I know, but Gideon loves it so, and I don't have the heart. Five years of marriage can't be destroyed with a snap of the fingers and a piece of paper." Vanessa sighed ruefully. "The house is a fairly minor inconvenience, after all—except when he starts insisting I drop everything and run down there to take care of some minor hassle." She sighed again. "Sorry Jilly, I didn't mean to sound off. I just wish he'd buy me out. Gideon doesn't seem to understand that I really don't like Hatteras, especially in the off-season." She shrugged. "It's been eighteen months since the divorce, and we did agree to get the thing settled as soon as he'd got his affairs sorted out."

Jilly regarded her sympathetically. "I think you're too

soft, friend. I watched that marriage of yours deteriorate. I'm not saying Gideon's a bad man, but he did see you as an extension of himself and he's still doing it over the Hatteras house. And you're still allowing it."

Vanessa felt a familiar tension building between her shoulder blades, and knew it was a reaction to the truth in Jilly's words. It had taken her the last three years of her marriage to face that truth and to do something about it— but it still hurt. Resolutely, she threw off the dark memories—she was creating a new life for herself now. She grinned suddenly.

"Guess what, Jilly? I had a *very* interesting flight back."

Jilly returned the grin. "Interesting *good* or interesting *bad?*"

"Good, I think. You know what a sucker I am for a pair of laughing eyes?" She regarded her friend carefully over the rim of her glass.

"I wouldn't have said you were a sucker for anything, actually," Jilly remarked calmly. "And you've been running like a scared rabbit from *every* pair of interested eyes, laughing or not, in the last eighteen months."

Vanessa wrinkled her nose. "Touché... Well, I'm not going to have the opportunity to run to or from this particular pair. I don't even know the name that goes with them—at least, not beyond Jason," she added.

"That's some start." Jilly laughed. "Sounds impressive!"

Vanessa frowned. "Now that you mention it, he is impressive—very." Remembering, she put a hand up to her head. "He kept tidying my hair, Jilly!"

Jilly burst into a peal of laughter. "Are you telling me, Van, that he actually saw through that calm, collected exterior of yours?"

Vanessa laughed reluctantly. "I was not exactly calm and collected when we met." And I'm not now, either, she thought distractedly. She'd spent one hour talking to a complete stranger as if she'd known him all her life, had allowed him to assume an intimacy that was quite uncalled-for. And now, she could think only of when, if ever, he would fulfill his promise of another meeting. But did she really want to renew an acquaintance with a man who could so unsettle her? Gideon had affected her similarly—and with near devastating results.

"Bedtime, Jilly Greyson." Vanessa got to her feet determinedly. "You've got to be in court tomorrow and I've got to spend the day pushing paper. Enough of my adventures for one night!"

"I look forward to the next installment." Jilly grinned, laying an arm over Vanessa's shoulders and hugging her briefly.

"If there is one." Vanessa smiled, returning the squeeze.

Chapter 2

THANK GOODNESS TODAY was going to be an office day! Vanessa gazed irritably out of the kitchen window the next morning at a steady torrent of rain. She could hardly see across the river to Georgetown, and the Whitehurst Freeway was a nasty tangle of stop-and-go traffic. She toyed briefly with the idea of working at home, but she didn't have all the papers she needed to get the Patterson contract in order. At least she could dress for the weather—there was no one who had to be impressed by a dressed-for-success look today! Wearing faded jeans, emerald-green turtleneck sweater, an old, comfortable jacket, and a pair of galoshes over the inevitable sensible shoes, she headed through the driving rain for her car. The traffic was horrendous; no one in this city seemed able to drive competently unless the sun shone from a cloudless blue sky, she reflected, negotiating the Fiat into a tight spot in the underground garage of her office building.

"Good morning, Hilary," she greeted her secretary, making a gallant effort to sound cheerful as she shook her feet out of the galoshes inside the door to the simply furnished office.

"A wet one." Hilary smiled. "Did you get the Patterson contract?"

"Yes, but I had to stay up half the night to do so," Vanessa said ruefully. "Any calls?"

"One from a Carlysle Electronics," Hilary replied. "Oh, and a messenger just delivered this." She handed over a large, square, brown-paper-wrapped package.

"What on earth . . . ?" Vanessa fumbled with the heavy-duty tape. "Oh . . ." she murmured, as a slim, elegant black briefcase was revealed. The initials V. H. stood out clearly on the leather. She snapped the briefcase open and found just a small piece of paper inside with bold black writing: "Happy landings, firefly."

"What is it?" Hilary asked inquisitively.

"A present from a traveling companion," Vanessa answered quickly, and disappeared into her tiny inner office.

Now what? She sat down at her desk, examining the briefcase minutely. Nothing accompanied the gift but that cryptic message—no name, no address. Somewhere in this town there was a tall, broad-shouldered man with crinkly gray eyes, a wide, intelligent brow jutting beneath a wiry thatch of graying brown hair, a creamy voice, and a very determined sense of humor. But where? She certainly wasn't going to find out unless he was prepared to be discovered. He'd found her easily enough, though, and quickly—it was only ten o'clock. She shook her head in frustration. Mystery stories had never appealed to her and she didn't like being pushed around like a pawn on a chess board.

Hilary stuck her head around the door. "Van? I've got Carlysle Electronics on the line again. They want to make an appointment today for a consultation."

"Not today," Vanessa said firmly. "I'm not moving from this desk until quitting time."

The secretary disappeared, but within seconds the intercom on Vanessa's desk buzzed. "Look, I'm sorry, Vanessa, but the woman from Carlysle Electronics is very determined. I get the impression she's in fear and trembling of her boss. And it sounds like a sizable potential contract, too."

"But I'm not dressed for visiting clients today!" Vanessa sighed. "Oh, okay, I'll talk to her." She pressed the button. "Hello, this is Vanessa Harrington."

"Oh, Dr. Harrington, Mr. Carlysle has asked me to set up an appointment with you for twelve-thirty today. I do hope you can manage it. He's very anxious to see you and has to be out of town for the rest of the week."

Vanessa thought for a moment. Business was far from bad, but she couldn't yet afford the luxury of spurning a possibly lucrative contract just because she didn't feel like leaving the office and driving in the rain. If this Mr. Carlysle was so insistent, he'd just have to put up with her scruffy costume.

"Very well," she agreed resignedly. "Could you please give me directions?"

At noon she was battling through the rain along Lee Highway. Carlysle Electronics—an imposing, many-windowed building—appeared sooner than she'd expected on the left of the highway. Consigning all hostile drivers to the fiery depths, she edged herself into the left lane, ignoring the hooting car behind her.

She shot across the busy highway and into the large, very full parking lot. The only vacant space seemed miles away from the main entrance, and she cursed as she realized that she'd forgotten her galoshes and umbrella. It was all too easy to do with an underground garage at the office. Furious, she braved the downpour, feeling the pouring rain instantly drench her hair. Water ran down her face and inside the neck of her sweater as she ran pell-mell through the river that had once been a parking lot. An attempt to dodge an enormous puddle misfired, and she plunged in, ankle-deep.

Felling ridiculously conscious of the water dripping off her, of her soaked jeans clinging to her thighs, and of the scratchy dampness of her high turtleneck, Vanessa pushed open the heavy glass doors of Carlysle Electronics. How could she possibly attend a business meeting looking like this? Her hair was escaping in bedraggled tangles from its pins, and she looked around feverishly for a bathroom.

"Dr. Harrington?" a soft voice arrested her. "Please, come upstairs." Vanessa turned to a small gray-haired woman in an immaculate business suit, hurrying across the foyer toward her. "Mr. Carlysle is waiting for you."

"I'd like to tidy myself up a little first," she said mildly.

"Yes, of course, but please, right this way." The woman took her arm, urging her toward the elevator.

Vanessa felt an absurd urge to laugh. What on earth was going on here? The woman chattered nonstop, shooting Vanessa anxious looks as the elevator sped upward and came to a smooth halt at the tenth floor, where it opened immediately onto a large, comfortable reception area.

"This way, please." So many "pleases," Vanessa thought with a quiet smile as her arm was taken again. Assuming she was being shown to the ladies' room, she went willingly. A large door was opened, and she found herself in an imposing, luxurious office.

"Good heavens! What a drowned firefly!" The rich voice flowed over her and she glared in an intensity of fury at her erstwhile traveling companion.

"You!" The sharp exclamation was all she could immediately manage.

"Yes, me. Jason Carlysle, at your service, Dr. Harrington. You're very wet, you know?" The tall figure came out from behind the enormous desk, his smoky eyes brimming with laughter and his full lips curving over gleaming, even white teeth.

Vanessa bounced indignantly on the balls of her soaked feet. "You need to do something about that parking lot of yours," she spat out. "It's full of craters!"

"I'm sorry, but did you have to come out in this"—he gestured toward the window—"without a raincoat or even an umbrella?"

"I was not intending to go anywhere today," she hissed, anger overwhelming her as a sense of being outrageously manipulated hit her with full force. "How dare you? Pretending to want a consultation..." Words failed her, and she glared silently at the insultingly dry, immaculately groomed man who stood laughing at her.

"Hey, back up, Dr. Harrington. Who said anything about pretending?" He grinned. "My request was perfectly genuine. And you can't in all fairness blame me for your present rather, shall we say, bedraggled state."

Before she could reply, he strode across the room, disappearing through a narrow door in the far wall. He was back almost immediately, holding a large, fluffy towel.

"Let's see if I can made amends," he murmured softly—it was an attempt to mask his amusement that failed miserably. Before she could react, he was unpinning her hair, running gentle, disturbing fingers through the soaked strands as they came loose. The towel went around her head and the surplus water was efficiently massaged out of the wet tendrils. Her face was buried against a crisp white cotton shirt encasing a wide, deep chest, and the dull thump of his heartbeat resounded in the crimson blackness behind her closed eyes. She attempted to pull herself free, but the grip only tightened.

"Hold still, Dr. Harrington," he teased. "I'm nearly done now." But he took his time, whether intentionally or not, Vanessa didn't know; she knew only the strangely sensual feeling of the brisk but curiously gentle rubbing movements on her head, the smell and feel of his virile body in the warm darkness.

"There you go." The towel left her head and she brought herself upright.

"If you have a hairbrush in your purse, I'll straighten it out for you," he offered cheerfully. "You look a bit like the wild woman from Borneo right now!"

"I can brush my own hair, thank you," Vanessa said frigidly, hunting through her purse. "Do you have a mirror, by any chance?"

"In the bathroom," he said soothingly. "You might also want to get out of those wet clothes and take a hot shower. There's a robe in there. We can put your clothes on the radiators to dry."

"Oh, don't be ridiculous!" Vanessa exclaimed. "I'm not sitting in your office, in your bathrobe, in the middle of the day!"

Jason frowned and reached a long arm to grasp the neck of her sweater. "You're absolutely drenched! Apart from being wretchedly uncomfortable, that's also rather unhealthy. You'll catch your death of cold, and I really don't want that on my conscience." He smiled. "Come on, be practical about this, Dr. Harrington." The voice was gentle, cajoling even, but Vanessa refused to relent.

"I think I'd better leave," she said with quiet, frozen dignity.

"Come now, that's not very sensible, is it? After all the trouble and discomfort you went through to get here—and I have a substantial contract for you if you play your cards right."

"Just what do you mean by that?" she said dangerously.

"Why, that you have a program to sell, of course," he said innocently. "That's what you came here to do, isn't it?"

"Yes." She shook her head in frustration. "But I don't normally conduct business in a bathrobe."

"Well, neither do I, actually," he said amiably. "But these circumstances are a little unusual. I was going to take you out for lunch, but perhaps I'll get Mrs. Macy to order us something from the deli instead. Go take that shower and I'll send her off on her lunch break—no one will know, I promise."

It was so absurdly reasonable, Vanessa reflected. She was standing in the middle of his office, dripping and shivering like a drowned kitten. He seemed quite sincere about the work proposition, and she could do a much more convincing job once she was warm and dry and had some food inside her. Shrugging lightly, she went through the narrow door into a small, but very well equipped bathroom.

The hot shower was soothing; the plentiful array of towels thick and luxurious; the robe heavy and warm. Vanessa rolled up the too-long sleeves and surveyed her discarded clothing thoughtfully. She was *not* going to put her lacy bikini underpants over any radiator, that was asking too much! She pulled them on again, shuddering slightly as their dampness molded itself uncomfortably to her warmed flesh. But at least she didn't feel quite so vulnerable—it was worth the discomfort.

Vanessa emerged from the bathroom to see Jason, still smiling, laying out what looked like a veritable feast on the wide desk top.

"I'll take those," he instructed cheerfully, reaching for her soggy clothes with a determined ease that she was beginning to find familiar. He shook the garments out, draping them carefully over the slim radiators standing under the picture windows.

"You seem to have forgotten something," he murmured, turning toward her, his gray eyes carefully hooded beneath half-closed lids. The twitch of his lips, though, betrayed the laughter she knew would be sparkling in their depths. "Come now, Vanessa. Feminine undergarments ceased to faze me at least twenty years ago, and you don't strike me as the coy type."

"Oh, Lord!" She turned her back on him, sliding the damp panties off with considerable relief, then stalked over to the window and spread them in a free spot on the radiator.

"And now, let's eat and get down to business," Jason said briskly.

She padded barefoot across the carpeted floor and looked with some awe at the beautifully arranged array of food. "Do you always eat such a magnificent lunch?" She looked up quickly at the pop of a cork.

"Only when I'm with someone who seems in need of a little special sustenance. I hope you're not a puritan about a glass of wine at lunchtime?" He turned, smiling, from a cabinet under a wall of bookshelves, holding an open bottle of Puligny-Montrachet in one hand.

Vanessa raised a mental eyebrow. When Jason Carlysle decided to look after someone, he clearly didn't stint. It was a strangely comforting thought. "No," she responded carefully, "as long as it's only one. I can't afford to fall asleep in the middle of the afternoon."

"What, never?" He grinned, his eyes flicking seductively over her well-wrapped figure.

"I forgot to thank you for the briefcase," she remarked with forced casualness. "It was a nice thought, but quite unnecessary."

"Most gifts are," he replied coolly.

"Sorry, that was a little ungracious," Vanessa said contritely.

"That's all right." He smiled, pouring the wine into two slender glasses. "I realize you're at something of a disadvantage right now."

That, Vanessa decided wryly, was putting it mildly.

"Why don't you put some food on that plate and come sit down? It's not going to get filled just by looking at it." Jason's creamy voice stroked her again, the teasing note tantalizing her nerve endings. She piled smoked fish, cream cheese, and black olives onto the plate, took a fork, and turned toward the couch where Jason was seated.

He seemed very relaxed, with one arm resting casually along the back of the sofa. Vanessa decided quickly to sit in one of the chairs opposite. The robe parted to her knees as she did so. She pulled it together again, resting her plate firmly on the recalcitrant opening.

"So, Dr. Harrington, if I want to set up an employee-assistance program in this company, how do I go about it?"

"Hire me," she responded promptly, taking a forkful of fish.

"Persuade me." His voice was firm and businesslike.

"You'll have to give me some information first," she said equally firmly. "What kind of company is this? What are your problems? What kind of management structure do you have? Why do you think you want such a program?"

"Well, to answer your last question first, until I found myself saving a firefly from some nasty bruises last night, I didn't think I did want such a program," he said blandly.

"Would you stop calling me a firefly?" Vanessa said crossly. "I'm here to talk business."

"Firefly is a very appropriate name for you," Jason remarked, tossing an olive pit into the ashtray on the table in front of him. "You're a green-eyed, red-haired, flitting little lightning bug. Right now, I'd like to put you in a jar and watch you light up."

Vanessa choked on her wine, burying her face in her napkin until the spasm had passed.

"You are an utterly impossible man!" she fumed. "I'm going to get dressed and leave. You are *not* interested in any program, and I have better things to do with my time than listen to your particular brand of sexist teasing." She got to her feet rapidly, moving to put her half-full plate on the desk.

"Oh, sit down, Vanessa. I'm sorry if I teased you. I promise, not one more comment of that kind will pass my lips this afternoon. I won't even call you firefly, if you insist. And I *am* truly interested in this program."

She looked at him doubtfully. It was still a contract, after all.

"Come on, drink your wine, Vanessa. I always keep my promises."

"Very well." She resumed her seat. "But one more un-professional comment and that's it—understood?"

"Understood," he said gravely, but his eyes were hooded again, and suspiciously concentrated on his plate. "Ask your questions again," he prompted as Vanessa silently adjusted the robe.

She repeated her queries, and as he answered them she formed swift, preliminary opinions. Carlysle Electronics sounded like something of a mess—top-heavy in middle-management, not enough delegation, an excess of absen-teeism.

"How long has this been going on?" she asked eventu-ally, wondering if the deplorable state of the company owed anything to its relaxed chairman lounging on the couch across from her.

"Years, I should think," he replied readily enough. "I took over two months ago. This is a fairly small branch of Carlysle Enterprises and was run by an uncle of mine until its general lack of production became so pronounced the family felt the need to do something about it."

"The family?" she echoed.

"Well, me, actually." He flashed her a disarming smile. "I've been running the whole show for the last ten years, but left this particular can of worms alone in the interests of family peace."

"So, how did Carlysle Electronics react to the big boss's arrival?" Vanessa asked, sipping her wine thoughtfully.

"Not too well, I'm afraid," he answered ruefully. "I've

been cracking the whip since I got here."

"So that explains poor Mrs. Macy," she murmured.

He laughed again. "You noticed, eh?"

"Hard to miss." She grinned.

"Maybe whip cracking isn't the answer," he said seriously. "You said some interesting things last night. I'm not entirely in sympathy with your philosophy, as I suspect you gathered, but I'm willing to give it a try."

"I'm very expensive," Vanessa stated unequivocally, no longer conscious of her unconventional clothing or even the disconcerting presence of Jason Carlysle. Her mind was totally occupied with the problems he'd presented; this was going to be a tough nut to crack.

"I didn't imagine you came cheap," he quipped. "How expensive?"

"That depends on how long it takes for me to familiarize myself with the setup," she replied. "I work for a retainer and expenses until I decide what's involved, then I present you with a contract outlining the program and you decide whether you want it or not."

"Okay, Dr. Harrington—tell me the worst. What's your retainer?"

"Two thousand dollars a week if I'm around full-time," she responded promptly.

"Whew! That is expensive, Dr. Harrington," he breathed.

"I gave you my credentials yesterday," she said quietly.

"So you did," he concurred briskly. "How do you want to work this?"

"I need an office, a typewriter—preferably a word processor . . ." He nodded in swift agreement. "And a memo from the management to go out to all staff members individually explaining exactly why I'm here, what I'm going to be doing, and what you hope to achieve by this exercise. I'll write the memo for you, of course," she went on, "but you'll have to approve and sign it."

"I get to do that much?" he murmured. "You certainly know what you want, Vanessa."

"You'd hardly employ me if I didn't," she retorted smartly.

"Very true. Why don't I show you a couple of empty

offices and you can decide which you'd prefer." He got to his feet and Vanessa rose enthusiastically, heading for the door.

"Hey!" His laugh arrested her. "You can't go out of here dressed like that."

"Oh!" She stopped dead. How on earth had she forgotten? That wretched single-mindedness of hers!

"Catch!" He moved toward the radiators and began to throw her clothes across to her. Socks, panties, jeans, jersey—she caught them all with automatic, instinctive movements, unable to halt the swift trajectory of her garments following each other without pause through the air.

"Play baseball, do you?" He laughed, his eyes crinkling beguilingly again.

"I used to," she responded briefly. His gaze suddenly—almost involuntarily, it seemed—dropped, fixed on the soft swell of her breasts, now exposed as a result of her swift reactions. Her own eyes followed his, became riveted on the V of skin revealed by the loosened robe.

"Better put those clothes on, Vanessa." The smooth, rich tones cut huskily through the tension and Vanessa went rapidly into the bathroom.

Her clothes were dry but crumpled, her hair impossibly tangled—only shampoo and conditioner could restore it to anything like its normal state. She twisted it into a chignon again and looked around for the pins. They were presumably in the office, where Jason had removed them earlier. Still holding her hair up, she went back.

"Where did you put my hairpins?"

"Here. Shall I do it for you?" He grinned, coming over to her, pins in hand.

"You seem to be making something of a habit of it," she retorted with a slight, resigned shrug.

"Well, I'm very experienced," he said lightly, those disturbing fingers in her hair again. "My ten-year-old daughter has hair halfway down her back and has to put it up for ballet class."

Vanessa's heart seemed to reach her toes with the sickening speed and thump of an out-of-control elevator. Fortunately, Jason was still occupied with her recalcitrant locks and she was able to keep her head down as she fought for composure. Why should it be such a shock? There had been no promises between them—he just had a flirtatious manner, apparently.

Realizing that she had missed the continuation of his remarks, she said, "Pardon? I didn't hear you."

"I said Emily lives with her mother most of the time— I just seem to get stuck with the ballet class once a week. I have a suspicion that's because it's not Emily but her mother who believes in the advantages of ballet, and I am a little more . . . uh . . . persuasive when it comes to getting Emily to do something she doesn't want." He released her with a final twist and the firm insertion of a pin. "There you go. Not exactly perfect, but the best I can do in the circumstances."

"Thanks." Vanessa absorbed his information without further comment. Had she detected a slightly strained note in that usually relaxed voice? She reached for her jacket—the soaking had done nothing to improve its originally shabby appearance.

"Ready, then?" Jason started toward the door.

"Hold on, Jason," she said quickly. "I look dreadful. I really don't want to make my first official appearance, as it were, looking as if I've just been dragged through a hedge backward."

He shook his head, frowning. "I'm going to be out of town for the rest of the week and I really want to set this up today. Tell you what—we won't make any introductions; I'll whisk you through the building, you can choose your office, tell me what you want in it, then come back here and draft that memo. *If* I approve it"—he grinned—"it can go out this evening and the staff will have the rest of the week to absorb it before you start on Monday."

"Hey," Vanessa interjected, her hands unconsciously resting on her hips. "What makes you think I can start on Monday? You're not my only client."

A long finger snaked out, touched her jutting, challenging chin, applied sufficient pressure to bring her face into alignment again, then was instantly removed.

"When *can* you start, Dr. Harrington?" he asked politely.

Vanessa swallowed. She wasn't used to having her challenges dismissed so easily, so casually.

"I can't start full-time next week," she said finally. "I have another contract to finish up, but I'll come in half days and do the preliminary work. Will that be all right?"

"Whatever suits you," came the courteous response. "Shall we go?"

His arm rested casually across her shoulders as he moved her swiftly through the building, indicating the various departments. He poured out information at such a clip that she needed all her concentration to take it in and quickly forgot her embarrassment at her scruffy appearance.

Back in his office, she took a legal pad out of her new briefcase and swiftly drafted the memo. It was the first step in any job—an initial attempt to break the ice and acquaint everyone concerned with some idea of what was going to happen and why. But it had to come officially from the management to show their commitment to the program.

Jason took the memo from her and read it slowly, with a deepening frown. "You really expect me to sign this?" he asked finally, looking across the desk.

"Yes," she replied flatly. "It's the truth, isn't it?" The memo stated clearly and unequivocally what problems existed in the company and laid them squarely at management's door. It also gave a brief description of employee-assistance programs and explained exactly what she would be doing and why.

"I suppose it is." He sighed. "But do we have to be quite so definite about whose fault all this is?"

"That's the way I work. You start on the basis of absolute honesty," Vanessa said bluntly. "If you have a problem with that, I'm the wrong person for your company."

"No negotiation on this one?" he queried, one eyebrow raised.

"'Fraid not."

"You're a very tough lady," he commented with a sigh.

"You wouldn't say that if I were a man!" she exploded.

"That was a thoroughly sexist remark."

"Now how could that be construed as sexist?" he mused, tapping his even white teeth with the top of his pen. "It was a mere statement of fact. You are tough, you are female. I'm very happy to substitute 'woman' for 'lady,' but I can't see that it makes much difference."

Vanessa glowered at him. Jason Carlysle was playing with her again, but he was so slippery she couldn't seem to get a hold on him for more than a minute.

"I'll have Mrs. Macy type this up," he said after a short silence. "Then I'll sign it and she can have it photocopied and sent around. She's going to have some fun with it—the phones will be ringing off the hook throughout the entire building."

Vanessa watched his broad back disappear into the outer office, then turned toward the window. It was still raining. An awful lot seemed to have happened since she'd arrived at La Guardia yesterday evening, and yet on paper it was just a new contract.

"Will you have dinner with me this evening?" A hand rested with shocking suddenness on her shoulder and she spun around, startled out of her reverie.

"I didn't hear you come back." She attempted a smile.

"That was obvious," he responded softly. "I don't know what you were thinking, but it certainly had your full attention."

"It was nothing of any importance," she said lightly, moving away from the warm pressure of his hand. Her body was behaving traitorously and her heart was thumping in the most ridiculously erratic fashion.

"Well, will you?"

"Have dinner with you?" She smiled brightly.

Jason merely looked at her intently.

"Yes, I'd like to," she said simply.

"Good. I'll pick you up at seven-thirty. Now, let me find you an umbrella."

Chapter 3

"GIDEON, I TOLD YOU, if the roof needs seeing to you'll have to deal with it yourself! You're the one who's insisting on keeping the house." Vanessa couldn't prevent herself from stamping one exasperated bare foot on the living room carpet as she faced her ex-husband that evening. As usual, he looked slightly harried, but the studied casualness of his jeans and open-necked shirt, and the ruffled hair that made him look as if he had just come in out of a gale were, she knew, carefully calculated to create just that impression.

"Look, Van, please be reasonable . . ." the clipped voice began.

"I am! You're the one who is being totally irrational and self-centered! It is not convenient for me to go to Hatteras right now, and you have a nerve demanding that I do so!"

"Oh, Lord!" Jilly's soft exclamation had them both whirling toward the door.

Vanessa's jaw dropped. Jilly she had expected to see, but not the tall, elegant figure behind her. Surely it wasn't seven-thirty yet? She had so wanted to greet Jason Carlysle with a calm air of sophistication for once. The first time she'd met him, she'd been about to sprawl in an undignified heap on her backside, and the second time she had looked like a drowned rat! Now she was standing in the middle of the room with her wet hair wrapped in a thick towel, turbanlike above her makeupless face. At least the bathrobe she was wearing fit her this time!

"I happened to meet your roommate at the door," Jason's rich voice murmured in soft apology. "I didn't mean to take you by surprise."

"I'm sorry. I'm not ready yet," Vanessa declared lamely.

"So I see," Jason concurred smoothly, but the laughter was there again. "I seem to have interrupted something." He glanced interrogatively at Gideon, who, to Vanessa's indignation, returned a slight, conspiratorial half smile, a small shrug, as if to say, "Women!"

"Look, I'm really sorry. I got back to the office and the phones were going berserk and Hilary had gone home and then I got home and Gideon turned up . . ." She waved her hands around in expressive frustration.

"Stop flitting, firefly! There's no hurry. I can come back in a half hour, if you like." The voice was soft but curiously firm and somehow contrived to ground Vanessa, to bring her down from the flagpole of her irritation and frustration.

"There's no need for that. Let me get you a drink." She moved swiftly to the bar. "I'm sure Jilly will play hostess while I get dressed." Jason smiled warmly at Jilly, who, Vanessa noticed crossly, was having considerable difficulty keeping a straight face.

"Of course," Jilly said promptly. "For heaven's sake, Van, go get ready."

"I'm going." Vanessa moved toward the door. "Oh, by the way—Jason Carlysle, Gideon Clarke." She waved a brief introductory hand and left them to work things out for themselves.

Her long red-gold hair sprang out in shining waves under the application of hairbrush and blow dryer, curling softly in a well-cut bob on her shoulders. The gentle greens and golds of the print shirtwaist dress accentuated and deepened the emerald of her slightly slanted eyes; its classical style drew attention to her slender waist, the soft curve of her hips, and long legs, as the material swung easily around her to midcalf. A pair of totally unsensible strappy sandals and a ridiculously small, impractical shoulder bag completed the outfit. She examined herself critically in the mirror, wondering whether the slim, creamy column of her neck rising from the deep V of her dress required any adornment. She grinned to herself and reached into the cabinet above the built-in dresser. A small opal pendant hung to the almost but not quite revealed cleft of her breasts. She nodded, satisfied, and went back into the living room.

"My, my," Jason murmured, crossing the room toward her. "I thought only leopards could change their spots. It seems fireflies can, too."

"They don't have spots," she said lightly, feeling her nipples lift and swell under the caressing scrutiny of his crinkly eyes. Molten gold spread through her belly and down her thighs.

"Look, Van, before you go, we have to reach an agreement about that roof." Gideon's insistent accents broke the mood and she turned on him.

"Gideon, I will *not* go to Hatteras in March, and you cannot browbeat me into it! I pay my share of the costs, and you can do any nursemaiding!"

"Vanessa, I told you I have to go away on business tomorrow."

"That's your problem, Gideon. I also have a job to do, you may remember. Jason, shall we go now?" Vanessa turned on her heel and marched into the hall, grabbing her wool coat from the closet on the way to the front door.

Jason closed the door quietly behind them and followed her impetuous progress down the hallway in silence.

Vanessa stopped suddenly. "I'm sorry, that wasn't very entertaining, was it?"

"Oh, I don't know," he said evenly. "Does it happen very often? I believe in the principle that forewarned is forearmed, you see," he explained, struggling to keep his lips from curving into that devastating smile.

"Only with Gideon." She grinned ruefully. "We've been divorced for a year and a half and he *still* behaves as if I have nothing better to do than run the domestic errands that he's too busy to do for himself."

"I had rather assumed he wasn't your brother." The voice throbbed with barely suppressed laughter.

"What a dreadful thought!" Vanessa gazed at him,

horror-struck. "Fancy being tied to Gideon by family obligations! Thank heavens, the only thing that keeps us in any sort of contact at the moment is that damn house."

Jason gave up the struggle and collapsed helplessly against the wall. "Your face is an absolute picture!" he gasped. "You are such an extraordinary mixture of awesome competence and endearing absurdity!"

"I am not absurd," she protested, fighting her own laughter now. "You've just always caught me at a disadvantage. Most people find me rather alarming, actually."

"Oh, well, I've never been frightened of lightning bugs," he said easily. "Are we going to spend the rest of the evening propping up this wall or shall we go eat?"

As he led her to his car, Vanessa raised her eyebrows slightly at the gun-metal Mercedes. Carlysle Enterprises obviously provided its chairman with a good living. When they reached the restaurant, Tiberio's, she noted the deferential way the maître d' greeted Jason before showing them to a booth in a quiet corner.

"Are you still attracted to that ex-husband of yours?" Jason asked conversationally, not raising his eyes from his intent study of the wine list.

"What sort of a question is that?" she responded swiftly.

"A straightforward question," he replied blandly. "To be answered or not, as you choose."

The waiter appeared opportunely and Jason gave their order with the quiet, courteous, commanding self-confidence that seemed such an intrinsic component of his personality. The waiter gave a slight bow and left them.

"Well, do you?" Jason sat back in his chair, regarding her steadily, his usually laughing eyes now serious.

"Do I what?" she prevaricated.

"Look, Vanessa, we played this game last night. Do you choose to answer my question or not? And don't say, 'What question?'"

"I wasn't going to." Vanessa took a roll from the napkin-covered basket, broke it carefully, spread it with sweet butter from the earthenware crock, and popped a morsel in her mouth. How could he possibly have guessed how important that aspect of her marriage had been? And how ultimately destructive, considering that the potent chemistry was all there was left.

"Gideon's a very attractive man," she said quietly. Jason nodded, waiting. Vanessa sighed, fiddled restlessly with her butter knife. What was she supposed to say, for heaven's sake?

"Doesn't that answer your question?" she managed eventually.

"Perfectly," he responded levelly. "I think you're entitled to ask a personal question, now."

"You mentioned your daughter this afternoon," she said tentatively.

"Ah, yes." He smiled softly, tenderly. "My not-so-little Emily. Well, she's ten years old; her mother and I have been divorced for five years. She spends at least one night a week with me, as well as alternate weekends and half the holidays. In spite of a fair degree of paternal prejudice, I have to admit that she is, on occasion, a spoiled brat." He sighed suddenly. "Her mother indulges her hopelessly and then sends her to me when she can't handle her anymore. It doesn't make for sweetness and light in our relationship, as I'm sure you can imagine." He broke off as the waiter arrived with their first course.

Vanessa nodded; then, deciding that she'd heard enough for one night, turned her attention to her baked clams. "Tell me about Carlysle Enterprises. You said you'd been running it for the last ten years?"

"Mmmm. Since I attained the wisdom and maturity of my thirtieth year." He chuckled. "I've become a lot wiser in the intervening years, I can tell you."

Vanessa joined his laughter. He was a delightful companion and she was feeling incredibly pampered. The clams disappeared, to be replaced with succulent trout, crisped with almonds and swimming sinfully in butter.

"How old are you, Vanessa?" The question took her by surprise, coming as it did totally out of the blue in the short silence that followed his detailed description of the family-owned corporation.

"Thirty. Why?"

He looked at her steadily, sipping the crisp white Burgundy that had accompanied their trout. "Just interested. *You* interest me."

Vanessa swallowed convulsively in the short, suddenly intense silence. "It wouldn't have been hard to guess," she said, with a light laugh. "You must have a pretty good idea if you add up all those years I spent in school."

Jason made no response and she drew in her breath sharply. A change had come over his face. It was no longer humorous; the full lips had suddenly tightened, the light-gray eyes darkened, and a deep, unmistakably sensual intensity had chased away the laughter.

"I want to make love to you, firefly." The velvet voice seemed to stroke the clothes from her body. She shivered suddenly. They seemed to be the only two people in the room—in the universe itself. What was happening to her? She was melting, becoming malleable, a soft object to be molded into shape by those long-fingered, sensual hands resting on the snowy linen of the table. But she couldn't allow it to happen. Not now, not yet, not ever again.

She needed to reply . . . and quickly; something to break the silence that seemed to stretch thinner and thinner between them.

"I don't make it a habit to pick up strange men at airports and fall straight into bed with them." Her voice sounded strange, colder than she'd intended—but that was probably all to the good. If she could muster some anger it would be even better. Jason Carlysle was altogether too much: too smooth, too confident—and he spent altogether too much time laughing at her.

He wasn't laughing now. "There's an implication there, Vanessa, that I don't much care for."

"Then I'm sorry, but you started this," she retorted sharply. "I don't know what kind of person you think I am, but whatever impression you've got, it's quite clearly the wrong one."

His sharp intake of breath grated in the tense silence like chalk on a blackboard. The gray eyes—without a trace of humor now—narrowed, the full lips tightened in a hard, straight line.

"Just what is all this about, Vanessa? I've spent quite long enough in this world to know when my attraction to a woman is reciprocated. You have a very revealing face."

"That has absolutely nothing to do with it. I met you twenty-four hours ago, and since then you've manipulated and controlled everything that's happened. But it's time you realized, Mr. Carlysle, that I do *not* jump on command! How dare you assume, on the basis of a few hours' acquaintance, that my 'revealing face,' as you put it, means anything more than that I find you moderately attractive? As far as I am concerned, we have a business contract and tonight's dinner is simply a confirmation of that arrangement." She was truly angry now and found herself continuing without pause, "I have been moderately attracted to many men I work with, and they have not automatically assumed that I was therefore prepared to leap into bed with them. Now, if you'll excuse me, I'll take myself home."

"If you insist upon leaving before I've finished my trout, Dr. Harrington, then by all means, let's go." Jason raised one finger in an almost imperceptible movement that nevertheless brought their waiter to the table immediately. "Check, please," he said briefly.

"There's no need for you to interrupt your dinner," Vanessa said frigidly. "I am perfectly able to get myself home without assistance."

"I don't doubt it," Jason replied calmly. "But when I invite a woman to dinner I like to see her to her door afterward. Your particular brand of Victorian morality should surely make that understandable."

Vanessa gasped. "And just what is that supposed to mean?"

"I am not prepared to deal with hypocrisy." The usually smooth, rich voice was now sharp and clipped. "I happened to say that I would like to make love to you—you'll be relieved to know, I'm sure, that I've since changed my mind. It was a statement from one experienced adult to another, but I obviously got the signals wrong. Sorry."

Vanessa sat quietly, concentrating on slow, deep breathing. She could, of course, leap to her feet and run, but that was hardly appropriate behavior for a thirty-year-old. She'd created the anger for a good reason—it certainly took the edge off passion! Now, she had simply to close the evening, and the relationship, with firm courtesy—lucrative contract or not. She got to her feet as Jason pushed his chair back. In silence, they gathered up coats, smiled polite good-byes and thank-yous to an attentive maître d', and went out to the parking lot.

They drove in silence through town, over Key Bridge, to Arlington, and into the garage of Vanessa's condominium building. She had expected Jason to drop her off at the main entrance and had her good-night speech prepared, but instead, still in silence, he parked, got out, came around, and opened the door for her with frozen politeness.

"Thank you for driving me back, but I can assure you I'm not about to get mugged between here and the lobby," she said quietly. "I'm sorry things had to end like this"—the prepared speech came easily now—"but accidental meetings rarely lead to successful relationships. I wish you all success with Carlysle Electronics."

Such a dignified, reasonable speech—but it didn't receive the response it deserved. In fact, it received no response at all! Jason merely took her arm in a firm clasp, easing her between the lines of parked cars toward the main entrance.

"This is quite far enough!" Vanessa pulled away from his grasp as they reached the door.

"I intend to see you home," Jason said curtly.

Short of telling the security guard that she had an unwelcome visitor, there was little she could do to stop him. In rigorous silence, they stood in the empty elevator, stepped out into the deserted hallway, and walked to her door. Now what? Vanessa felt for her key in her purse. She'd tried twice to bring this evening to a polite, mature close and been blocked each time. She was all out of ideas at this point.

She was not prepared for the firm hands taking her face, tilting it upward so her gaze seemed to lose itself in those gray pools.

"I'm going to kiss you good night, firefly," the soft voice warned. His thumbs stroked lightly over her eyelids, the tips of his fingers sliding under her hair, tracing the outline of her ears, circling the vulnerable spot behind the lobes.

"You are not!" she protested fiercely, trying to draw back.

"I've been kissing my dates good night since I was fourteen," Jason stated matter-of-factly. "I'm not about to stop now."

"I am *not* your date, Jason Carlysle—never have been and never will be. Would you please let me go?"

"In a minute. I want to be sure of something first."

His hands continued to hold her, and she was waiting breathlessly for something to happen; but his gently curving lips kept their distance while his long fingers continued to play their tantalizing dance over her face, her ears. She couldn't control the wild fandango of her pulses, the liquid sensation in her lower body. And still he didn't kiss her.

"I'm quite sure now," the creamy tone stroked softly. "I don't need that kiss."

Involuntarily, Vanessa gasped, her mouth opening on the sharp inhalation of disappointment, and then he was covering her face with his; a strong but gently exploring tongue plunged inside her inviting lips, slipping around her teeth, caressing the softness of her cheeks, drawing her tongue against his, and then inside his own mouth. He tasted sweet and wonderful, of wine and laughter. Of their own volition, her hands slipped beneath his jacket, ran over the muscled back, stroked the knobbly spine, the sharp shoulder blades, pulled him tighter against her, feeling his desiring hardness against her taut thighs.

He drew away then, loosing her head, moving his hands to her shoulders, pushing her away from him, smiling down at her flushed face. "Next time we'll see if we can reach second base! Good night, Vanessa."

Without another word, he turned on his heel and strode off down the hallway, leaving Vanessa staring after him. She was getting in deep water again, in spite of all the promises she'd made to herself in the last year. After the divorce, when she'd faced the humiliating fact that however incompatible she and Gideon were she could still imagine making love with him with the old pleasure, she had sworn to take any future relationships very slowly. She had painfully learned that strong physical attraction didn't automatically lead to shared interests, relaxed companionship, good conversation. It was all too easy to mistake the one for the other initially, but she was not going to make that mistake again.

Her door key slipped from the grasp of her suddenly uncoordinated fingers and in frustration she leaned on the doorbell.

"What's the matter?" Jilly flung open the door, gazing at her in alarm.

"I'm sorry if I woke you, Jilly," Vanessa muttered, stumbling through the doorway. "I'm all at sixes and sevens!"

Jilly began to laugh. "Van, you are *so* funny sometimes. Has that enchanting Jason Carlysle got under your skin?"

"And how!" Vanessa sighed, dropping onto the couch. "But I'm not ready for anything yet. All I want is some relaxed, undemanding male companionship."

"Did you tell him that?" Jilly regarded her closely.

"Sort of—but not very subtly," Vanessa confessed.

"Well, apart from the fact that he is absolutely the sexiest man I've ever laid eyes on, including my adored Tom," Jilly stated with conviction, "I got the impression that he'd be quite willing to make the effort to understand you." She gave a sudden snort of laughter. "I love that 'firefly' bit. It's so absolutely right!"

"Oh, don't," Vanessa groaned. "I'm going to be working with him for the next however-many weeks, and he has the strangest effect on me. He's such good company, if only I can manage to keep it on that level." She gave another deep sigh. "I'm half inclined to back out in sheer self-preservation."

The uncomfortable thought hung in the back of her mind that her attempts to back out so far had not been crowned with success.

Chapter 4

VANESSA DRESSED WITH great care for her first morning at Carlysle Electronics. She needed to look smart but not intimidating, businesslike but approachable—a well-tailored brown mohair skirt with deep pockets and a discreet front split, and a gold silk shirt with full sleeves and tight wrists seemed to create the impression she wanted. How she was going to deal with Jason Carlysle she didn't know, but she swung through the heavy doors punctually at nine o'clock on a beautiful Monday morning with her usual confident optimism. She'd dealt with tougher come-ons than Jason's over the years.

A call from Mrs. Macy last week had confirmed the arrangements she'd made with Jason—one week half-time, then full-time until she was ready to present him with her findings and a draft program. The secretary had asked her to go straight up to Mr. Carlysle's office on her arrival, and with brisk determination Vanessa emerged from the elevator at the tenth floor.

"Good morning, Dr. Harrington." Jason turned from the secretary's desk where, still wearing his coat, he was leafing through a pile of papers.

"Good morning, Mr. Carlysle," she reponded formally. His gray eyes flicked over her, crinkled at the corners again; his lips curved slightly.

"Come on in. Mrs. Macy, could you rustle up some

coffee for us?" He opened the door to his office, held it for her as she walked past him. She hadn't seen him since that evening, and in the interim had attempted to arm herself to resist him, but the magnetism of his physical presence was threatening to drive all else from her mind.

She watched as he took off his coat, hung it neatly in the closet, perched himself on the corner of his desk.

"How are you, firefly?" he asked softly. "Ready for second base?"

Vanessa inhaled sharply. "I am prepared to fulfill my contract."

He laughed. "I think I'm going to have to kiss you again, my memory's fading. Why don't you come over here?"

"I'm staying right where I am," Vanessa declared firmly.

"What a pity." Jason gave an exaggerated sigh. "But still, I can wait—can you, Vanessa?"

"Would you stop it?" she hissed indignantly. "I told you before that I would not be teased like that, and you agreed."

"So I did," Jason acknowledged reluctantly. "But actually that was only for that one day—we have to renegotiate now."

Vanessa, really angry now and grateful for it, pushed her hands deep in the pockets of her skirt and strode across the room toward him.

"Mr. Carlysle, let's get one thing straight, once and for all." She spoke with fierce, quiet emphasis. "When I take on a job, I work for my fee and I work hard, and the fact that I happen to be a woman is a matter of total irrelevance. I will not play either sex games or sex politics when I'm working. Is that clear?"

"You're doing it again," he said calmly, laying a firm finger on her outthrust chin, pushing it down. "I have one really dreadful failing," he went on plaintively.

"Only one?" Vanessa exclaimed, stepping back hastily from that finger.

"Well, several actually, but this one's the most inconvenient." He grinned. "I'm always impossibly attracted to the most bossy, domineering women. I can't understand it, can you?"

Her mouth opened before she could find words to put in it and he slid off the desk with a purposeful movement. Remembering what had happened the last time she'd opened her mouth like that, she backed away just as the door opened and with a clatter of cups Mrs. Macy bustled into the room.

Vanessa exhaled softly and went over to the window, gazing with intense concentration at the parking lot and the busy highway.

"Interesting view, isn't it?" Jason said politely, a hint of laughter behind the words. "Do you take cream and sugar in your coffee?"

"Just cream, thanks." She turned to take the cup with hands that were not quite steady. The gray eyes were brimming with amusement. Wretched man! she thought furiously; he was inviting her silently to join in the joke and she couldn't resist. Her lips twitched slightly and she took a quick gulp of the very hot coffee, scalding her tongue.

"All right, Vanessa, you're off the hook now." His deep voice came soothingly across to her. "Only business in the office, I promise. Now, shall I give you a real tour and introduce you to the key people, or do you want to go it alone?"

"No, not at all," Vanessa said swiftly. "It will be a help if you take me around—your staff needs to know that you're behind the idea; that you're interested in the problems and really want to find a solution that's in their best interests."

"I thought that memo was supposed to do that." He grimaced.

"You need to back it up with your active support," she said quietly.

"I'm at your service, Dr. Harrington," Jason said and bowed her out of the office.

They spent about two hours touring the building, with Jason introducing her to everyone whose support and co-operation might be important for her. Vanessa noted a strong reluctance among the staff to talk openly to her at this point and wondered how much of it had to do with Jason's presence and how much with the natural wariness accorded anyone operating under top management's umbrella. Jason seemed very easy and relaxed, however; he knew most people's names and usually managed some personal comment or question—he had obviously gone to some trouble to get to know his staff, she reflected with interest. She kept her own questions and comments casual, trying to establish the base of friendliness and trust without which the task facing her could not be accomplished.

There was a fair degree of inevitable suspicion. She was going to have to win over the union, which saw her as another piece of managerial interference, but it was always that way at first. The biggest problem was going to be with middle management—they had too much invested in the status quo to welcome any changes.

Jason walked her back to her office after their tour. "Have you got everything you need in here?" He gestured around the simply furnished room. "It looks a bit bare."

Vanessa shook her head in a quick disclaimer. "No, it's fine. All I need are those two comfortable chairs in case anyone decides voluntarily to come talk to me—it does happen sometimes!" She grinned. "And a desk and the word processor. I'm grateful for that, by the way, it'll halve my work."

"Why don't you use a dictaphone and I'll allocate you a secretary?" He frowned.

"Jason, you're not going to want anyone but you seeing my initial report," she stated bluntly.

"That sounds alarming." He sighed. "Well, don't leave without saying good-bye, will you?"

"Checking up, are you?" Vanessa mocked. "Perhaps you'd like me to punch that time clock in the hall?"

Jason shook his head at her reprovingly, clicking his tongue against his teeth. "I think you're going to have to pay for that, firefly," he promised softly. "But I'll exact the penalty at a rather more appropriate time and place."

By one o'clock, she'd got her initial impressions on paper and went thoughtfully upstairs again, holding her report in her hand.

"Jason, do you have a filing cabinet that locks?" she inquired as she walked into his reception area. He turned from his conversation with Mrs. Macy and waved her into his office, pointing toward the tall cabinet by the window. She found a vacant slot for the folder and closed the drawer with a decisive snap.

"That stuff's real dynamite, is it?" he questioned.

"Some people are not going to enjoy it," she said flatly. "It may sound a bit paranoid, but I've run into trouble before with the wrong people getting hold of the wrong pieces of paper."

"I'll get a cabinet put into your office this afternoon," he said simply. "Now, how would you like to meet Emily this evening?"

Whatever she'd expected, it hadn't been that.

"She's got ballet class," he went on with a smile, "so she won't be around *all* evening. I'll cook you a rather special dinner as compensation."

Vanessa regarded him thoughtfully. Jason Carlysle intrigued her, had somehow touched a chord that made her want to know much more about him. His behavior with the employees this morning had been quite at odds with his earlier suspicions of her liberalism when it came to worker/management relations, and that quiet but invincible authority of his seemed to go hand in hand with a capacity for tenderness and understanding that was both reassuring and immensely appealing. How would he be with his "not-so-little Emily"? There were problems there, that much he had hinted fairly broadly, but she remembered the way his eyes and voice softened when he spoke of the child.

"You seem to be having a problem with this, Vanessa." Jason's voice broke gently into her reverie.

"No, not at all." She smiled cheerfully, her mind made up. "I'd like to come very much. Just one thing, though . . ."

His thick brown eyebrows lifted interrogatively.

"You're not inviting me with any . . . hidden agendas?"

Jason grinned slightly. "You made your position very clear, Vanessa, and I don't usually need telling twice. I am a very patient man."

"You're going to need to be," she retorted sharply, too sharply.

He frowned. "Such vehemence! I wish I knew what was behind it."

"It's a long story," she said candidly. "But I didn't mean to bite your head off. What time this evening?"

"Six o'clock all right? I should have fought the homework battle by then, and Emily doesn't leave until six-thirty."

"Six is fine. Tell me where."

"Thirty-fifth Street." He wrote the chic Georgetown address on a memo pad.

"Until this evening then."

Jason Carlysle's house was in an elegant street of turn-of-the-century row houses, all immaculately kept. It took Vanessa a good ten minutes to find a parking space, but that was par for the course in this area. She ran through the blustery wind along the neat sidewalk, her hair in a careless ponytail flying behind her. She'd decided to team a pair of jeans with expensive knee-high leather boots and a smart, button-down silk shirt. She felt both dressed up and dressed down—it ought to do for an informal domestic supper. That was really all it was going to be—with a ten-year-old child around, Jason surely couldn't be intending to pursue his attack, and he had promised, after all. The cream-painted front door opened directly onto the sidewalk and she pressed the bell, peering at the elaborate black cast-iron door-knocker as she did so.

The door swung open under eager hands and Vanessa found herself being subjected to the scrutiny of a wide pair of very familiar gray eyes in a small, heart-shaped face.

"Hi. You must be Emily?" She smiled.

The head nodded vigorously, sending a wash of silver-blond hair rippling around the girl's face.

"You're Vanessa." It was a statement, not a question.

"That's right."

"Well, Daddy's upstairs." The child pulled the door wider. She was tall for her age but very slender, the leotard and tights accentuating the supple, girlish figure.

Vanessa, taking the opened door as invitation, walked

past Emily into a narrow, carpeted hallway.

"I had some of what you're going to have for dinner," the child's voice chimed cheerfully. "It's delicious. Daddy's a much better cook than Mama. Come upstairs."

Vanessa followed Emily as the child flew up the flight of stairs ahead of her, reflecting that while she hadn't known quite what to expect of Jason Carlysle's daughter, this silver-haired, gray-eyed sprite was not entirely a surprise.

Emily flung open the only door on the narrow first-floor landing, declaring, "Here she is."

Vanessa walked into an enormous room. A bright fire blazed in the hearth opposite her, heavy drapes were pulled across the bow windows facing the street. The near end was an elegant, book-lined living room; the far end a kitchen straight out of *House & Garden*. Jason turned from the counter and smiled. It was the first time she'd seen him in anything but a suit, and the sight of that masculine physique in well-cut, hip-hugging jeans and a casual knit shirt unbuttoned far enough to reveal gray-brown hairs curling on his broad chest took her breath away.

"Take this to Vanessa, will you, Emily? And then finish getting ready," the mellow voice instructed, as he held out a glass across the peninsular counter.

"What a gorgeous room!" Vanessa managed, once her pulse rate had slowed a little.

"Why, thank you, firefly." He laughed. "I like to cook but hate to do it alone—this arrangement solves that problem." He waved a hand around in a casual, descriptive gesture.

"It certainly does. Oh, thank you, Emily." She took the tulip-shaped glass of white wine with a smile.

"I like your shirt," the child commented thoughtfully. "That rusty color is almost exactly the color of your hair."

Vanessa inclined her head with a smile in gracious acceptance of what she assumed was a compliment.

Jason chuckled. "Emily's taste is, as always, impeccable. Run along, now, poppet, you can continue your examination of Vanessa when you're dressed."

The child grinned sunnily and left the room.

"Now," he continued cheerfully, "I'm up to my elbows in vegetables, so you'll have to come to me."

She crossed the room slowly—the magnet of those crinkly eyes drawing her toward him.

"Lift up your face—unless you want me to hold you with oniony hands."

She obeyed with a slight smile and received a warm, dry kiss on her lips. "That's just a promise," he whispered.

"Jason, I told you . . ." she began.

"Sure you did," he agreed smoothly. "But a man can hope, can't he?"

"Hey, break it up, you two," Emily's voice announced suddenly. "You've got to do my hair, Daddy."

Jason sighed. "You're a little too precocious for your own good, my child."

"Would you like me to do your hair, Emily?" Vanessa moved swiftly away from the danger zone. "I'm actually even more experienced than your father—in some things, at least," she added with a grin.

Jason gave a soft choke of laughter. "I'm keeping a tally of those remarks of yours, Vanessa. When the time's right, I'll have my revenge!"

Vanessa dumped herself into a velvet wing chair by the fire and gestured to the floor at her feet. "Why don't we braid it and make a crown, for a change?" she asked cheerfully, pulling the brush through the silky head resting against her knee. While she worked, Emily subjected her to a barrage of questions, many of them remarkably personal. Vanessa answered them as honestly as she could, conscious always of the quiet, attentive male figure in the kitchen behind her.

"Okay, go show Daddy," she announced briskly, securing the braids with a final pin in a neat coronet around the small, well-shaped head.

Jason examined his daughter with a mock-serious look, head tilted on one side. The child laughed delightedly and Vanessa's stomach seemed to somersault. They were remarkably alike.

"Better get your coat, poppet. Your ride will be here in

a minute." Jason bent to drop a kiss on his daughter's neat, shiny head.

"I don't want to go, my ankle hurts," the child declared suddenly.

"Oh, don't do this to me tonight, Emily, please!" Jason sighed wearily and turned back to his work.

"Mama doesn't make me go if I don't want to," Emily insisted petulantly.

"I am not your mother," Jason said firmly.

"That's obvious!" A small foot stamped.

"That will do, Emily. Get your coat."

"But I don't want—"

Jason turned swiftly, resting his hands on the counter at his back. "That will do, young lady. Now get your coat."

Vanessa took a quick sip of her wine and sank farther into her chair. That was a tone she had never heard from Jason Carlysle before. But it seemed his daughter had. With a look of frozen dignity on her face, Emily stomped out of the room. Vanessa turned slightly to look behind her. Jason was watching the rigid little back, a broad grin on his face. He winked at Vanessa.

"See what I mean? I told you my daughter is spoiled."

"She's very pretty," Vanessa remarked, getting up from her chair.

"True. She takes after her mother in more ways than one," he muttered.

"Your ex is pretty, then?" Vanessa asked casually, examining the books on one wall with considerable attention.

"Who, Diane? Oh, she's beautiful," Jason said, "but you know what they say about beauty being only skin-deep?"

The doorbell chimed loudly, saving Vanessa from the need to respond immediately. Jason wiped his hands vigorously and moved toward the door. "I'd better make sure Emily actually leaves," he said, laughing. "I wouldn't put it past her to tell the Camerons she's not feeling well tonight and then hide herself in her room—or listen outside the door, more likely!" He strode out of the room and Vanessa heard the cheerful greetings from downstairs, his easy, "Bye-bye, poppet. Have a good time." Then the door shut and there was a strange, waiting silence in the house.

"What happened with your marriage?" she asked, unable to prevent herself, as he came back into the room and went to throw another log on the fire. He was kneeling very close to her, the belted waist of his jeans gaping slightly at the back as he stretched forward. Vanessa had to resist the urge to slide her hand between the material and his skin. She knew how it would feel as vividly as if she were actually doing it.

He frowned, sitting back on his heels, then shrugged and got to his feet. "It's the old, old story. I was away a lot—too much, I admit. Diane is a real social butterfly; it was inevitable she'd find some compensation for her lonely nights." He went back into the kitchen.

Vanessa followed him, unable to leave the subject alone. "Were you very hurt?"

"Sure I was." The reply was swift and definite.

"Are you still hurt?" she persisted.

Jason turned then, taking her hands, pulling her toward him. "No, firefly, I am *not* still hurt. In fact, if it weren't for Emily, I'd be thanking my lucky stars for a narrow escape every day of my life. Satisfied?"

"I didn't mean to pry," she murmured, wondering why she couldn't breathe properly. Her eyes were fixed on the curling hair spidering between his shirt buttons. Would it be soft or coarse to the touch? If he weren't holding her hands quite so firmly, she'd be able to find out.

"You weren't prying, Vanessa. I only answer questions I choose to answer."

A sudden popping, hissing noise from the stove behind them stopped whatever was about to happen and Jason released her hands with a violent exclamation, turning to deal with the overboiling pot.

"Give me something to do," Vanessa said firmly. "I feel singularly useless just standing around here while you work."

"Light the candles, fill the glasses, and sit at the table," he instructed. "I was in danger of forgetting that this particular meal requires undivided attention!"

"Emily informed me that it was delicious," she said with a grin, striking a match.

"That child has champagne tastes," Jason declared. "As

I said, she takes after her mother." He brought a large bowl of steaming asparagus to the table. "This first." He piled her plate, handing her the bowl of hollandaise sauce to pour over the bright, tender stems.

"Now, bossy lady, how about a little reciprocal information?" He sat down opposite her, raising his glass in a light salute.

"I am *not* bossy!" Vanessa protested hotly.

"Oh, no? How else would you describe that performance of yours this morning?" He was laughing at her again.

"Now just hold on a minute! I was merely defending myself from a piece of blatant chauvinism," Vanessa retorted. "As you very well know!"

"You really do lead with your chin, Vanessa," he remarked mildly, leaning across the table, again pressing a firm finger against her determinedly jutting jaw.

"Let's talk about something else." Vanessa squirmed away from his touch. "I'm beginning to wonder why I'm here at all."

"Are you really?" he teased. "That seems remarkably blind."

Vanessa concentrated on her asparagus, studiously avoiding Jason's laughing eyes. "How was your trip, by the way?" she asked neutrally.

He chuckled. "Nice try, firefly." He picked up her empty plate and went back to the stove. "Actually, I think once you've finished with Carlysle Electronics I'm going to have to ship you off to the Kansas plant. All hell's breaking loose there, at the moment."

"Oh, tell me about it." She sat up, her interest quickening.

"You really do want to know, don't you?" He sighed, putting a savory, steaming bowl in front of her. "You're proving a lot harder to seduce than I thought you'd be."

"Cool it, Jason!" She glared at him. "You invited me for supper and to meet your daughter, remember?"

"I'll remember to be patient," he remarked. "On the principle that everything comes to him who waits. What do you think of my bouillabaisse?"

"It's delicious." Vanessa smiled, accepting the changed subject with relief. Surely, no man was irresistible—but then why did she find Jason Carlysle so difficult to resist?

"You are some cook!" Vanessa declared, leaning back in her chair, easing her hands into the suddenly tightened waist of her jeans.

He grinned. "It's a hobby of mine. Want more sorbet?"

She shook her head. "No, I couldn't."

"Well, that's all to the good," Jason remarked thoughtfully. "I promised to save some for Emily, but we seem to have eaten most of it!"

Vanessa laughed and began to clear away the dishes.

"Leave them, Vanessa. They'll get done in the morning," the rich voice ordered firmly. "Sit by the fire and I'll bring us some coffee."

"How can you possibly face all this in the morning?" she demurred, gesturing toward the littered table and kitchen.

"I don't have to. I have a splendid housekeeper. She'll have this all cleared away and Emily breakfasted before I appear at eight o'clock."

"In that case..." Vanessa shrugged and went over to the fire.

The sudden sound of the front door opening, then crashing shut, startled her. Had they really just spent two and a half hours over dinner?

"Did you save me some sorbet?" Emily's bright voice chirped as her slender figure hurtled into the room, bringing the cold air and the outside world with her in her pink, glowing cheeks and sparkling, inquisitive eyes.

"We did. You can scrape the bowl." Jason chuckled. "No, poppet! Not with your fingers!"

"But it tastes better that way." Emily grinned engagingly.

Jason laughed. "I know it does—I always used to think so when I was your age. You might at least take off your coat, though, and if you want to eat it by the fire with us you're going to have to use a spoon. I don't want sticky fingers all over the rug."

"Okay." Emily shrugged easily and complied, following

with the bowl as he brought the coffee tray over to the fire.
She questioned and chattered nonstop for the next half hour,
pausing only to scrape the last fragments of sorbet out of
the bowl with anxious determination. She was sitting on the
floor leaning against Jason's knees; one long finger absently
stroked her bent neck while his other arm lay casually along
the back of the couch. He didn't touch Vanessa's shoulders,
but she was continually conscious of that arm.

"Okay, poppet—you've had a half hour extension tonight. Now, off you go." The instruction was issued with
cheerful briskness.

Vanessa held her breath, wondering if he would be chal-
lenged. There was a short, tense silence. The seemingly
relaxed body next to hers appeared content to wait, but she
could sense the preparatory tensing of his muscles. Then,
with a heavy, exaggerated groan, Emily pulled herself to
her feet. "You are *so* old-fashioned, Daddy," she grumbled.
"Everybody gets to stay up until ten o'clock."

"Well, you, my love, are not everybody." He smiled.
"Say good night now."

Vanessa turned her head against the back of the couch,
watching as Jason drew the child between his knees, responding to the enthusiastic bear hug he received by holding
Emily tightly against his chest.

"Happy dreams and big ice creams, poppet," he said,
releasing her with what seemed to Vanessa a reluctant sigh.

Emily tightened her hold around his neck. "I won't let
you go," she declared fiercely against his cheek.

"No one's letting anyone go, my love," he said softly,
caressing the small face with the palm of one large hand.

Vanessa felt a rush of warmth for this man who was so
clearly able to read between the lines, to hear the real message behind the child's words and to respond with such calm
reassurance.

"Can I read in bed?" Emily drew herself upright, her
voice normal, cheerful, no longer intense.

"Just for ten minutes—it's late."

"Well, I'm not a bit tired," Emily declared stoutly, and
then totally failed to suppress a deep yawn. They all laughed.

"'Night, Vanessa." Quite unself-consciously, Emily leaned over and kissed her. Vanessa returned the embrace, feeling a sudden tug at her heartstrings, a sense of being incredibly complimented by her matter-of-fact inclusion in the goodnight ritual.

The door closed on the reluctantly departing figure and Vanessa held her breath again in the sudden silence. One of them had to make a move—it should be she and the move should be in the general direction of the door. A slow finger began to run down the bridge of her nose, traced the outline of her lips. Too late now, she thought distractedly.

"I think it's time for my revenge," Jason's chocolate-cream voice smoothed. "Don't you?"

"I have to go," she said, but somehow couldn't will herself to move. His fingers were caressing her throat now, his thumb and forefinger kneading the skin beneath her chin.

"Don't tell me you're going to be so impolite as to eat and run," he murmured. "It's early yet."

She couldn't say anything as his hand slipped gently down to the neck of her shirt, the fingers insinuating them-selves, feeling for her soft skin beneath the thin material of her shirt.

"Jason, don't. What about Emily?" she protested weakly.

"What about her? She's not going to come down again, if that's what you're afraid of—not unless it's an emer-gency."

The buttons on her shirt seemed to be coming undone almost of their own volition. Her head was resting against Jason's shoulder in the shelter of his firm arm as his fingers continued their gentle but implacable work. She had been made love to many times, but never with this total lack of urgency. Jason seemed quite content to hold her like this, looking into the fire, stroking the soft upper swell of her breast but reaching no farther although her nipples were now hard and tingling, longing for his touch. He brought his other hand around slowly, taking her chin between his long fingers.

"How are you bearing up, firefly?" his low voice mocked gently. "You can relax, you know. I promised to play this game at your pace. I have no desire to be subjected to another attack like the last one. You're going to have to ask for it when you're ready."

His lips came down on hers then, silencing whatever she had been about to say. He invaded, plundered, possessed her mouth with a strength and determination that was a far cry from the gentle sweetness of the last kiss and totally, crazily at odds with the still gentle fingers plucking and stroking her breast.

Her body began to respond, a slow tension building deep inside, filling her with warmth, with sweetness. Her hands lifted involuntarily to his head, her fingers ran through the soft, wavy thickness of his hair as her tongue fenced with his—touched, drew back, caressed. She was arching against his hard body now, moving her breasts against his gently stroking hands. At last she felt him cup the soft orb; a deliciously roughened fingertip tantalized the painfully hard crown and she moaned softly. For this moment there was no confusion, just the utter lucidity of Jason Carlysle's presence, of their wanting, needing bodies pressed close, of the overpowering sense of warmth and tenderness that this evening had engendered.

Slowly, his face left hers, hung above her, its contours coming at last into hard relief as the mists of passion receded.

"Oh, Vanessa, we *are* going to enjoy ourselves," he whispered. She was lying across his knee now, but incredibly, fantastically, his hands were carefully, deftly, buttoning up her shirt. Confusion now rushed upon her, engulfed and smothered her. What was he doing? What *had* he been doing? His teasing voice echoed in her memory: "Next time we'll see if we can reach second base." What sort of high school game did he think he was playing?

Fury took the place of passion. She leaped to her feet, pushing his hands aside, forcing the loosened shirt into the waist of her jeans with trembling fingers.

"You bastard, Jason Carlysle!" she hissed. "How dare you do that to me? How dare you manipulate me in that way!" Grabbing her purse, she headed for the door.

"Douse that light of yours, firefly," he said quietly. He

didn't move, but the readiness to do so was clearly obvious in the sudden tensing of his body. "You're not leaving here in that state. You'll be pressing the accelerator instead of the brake!"

Vanessa stopped halfway to the door, the logic of his statement seeping through gradually. Still, she hesitated.

"Come and sit down again," he continued softly. "I am very sorry. I really didn't intend that to happen. You are actually, Vanessa, even more passionate than I'd thought. I promise—no more games. Let's have some more coffee and finish the evening in a civilized manner."

Vanessa remained standing, irresolute, as she struggled to control her breathing and the wild pounding in her veins. "Just what were you trying to prove?" she asked tightly.

"I wasn't trying to prove anything," he replied evenly, leaning over the back of the couch to look at her. "Would you please come and sit down? I'm getting a stiff neck." She moved slowly to the wing chair by the fire.

"That's better," he continued. "Now, honestly, all I had in mind for this evening was for you to see me in my nonthreatening role of 'Daddy.' You're scared of something, and I hoped to prove to you that if it's me, you don't need to be. I had fully intended to give you a superb dinner, indulge in a little very light romance, and send you on your way with a good-night kiss that might have stirred you up a bit. But you took off like a kite in a tornado and things got out of hand. I tell you, firefly"—a husky note crept into his deep voice—"if it weren't for Emily upstairs, things would not have ended when they did."

"You mean you weren't doing it deliberately?"

"No, of course not, what on earth do you think I'm made of—agate?"

"But you said—"

"Oh, for goodness' sake, Vanessa!" he interrupted impatiently. "I was just teasing you a little. I still don't know what's behind this reluctance of yours to respond in a logical fashion to a very obvious attraction, but I have to assume it makes some sense to you—you don't strike me as particularly illogical."

"Sex isn't everything," she murmured.

"No, I don't think I'd quarrel with that," he commented, eyes resolutely fixed on the fire.

"You're laughing at me again," she accused, glaring at him.

"No, I'm not," he denied. "I'm merely waiting for you to give me the background. We've agreed that sex isn't everything, so? . . ." His eyes crinkled at her, and reluctantly she smiled slightly.

"I suppose that was a rather corny way of putting it," she admitted, examining her fingernails intently—how to explain this lucidly but without self-pity? She looked up with sudden decision. "I've been burned once by assuming that that particular kind of warmth and sharing was an off-shoot of the deeper, personal, basic warmth and sharing between two people—that physical love was merely an expression of the other. Somehow, although I still don't understand quite how, it seems that they can be separated. Or at least," she added miserably, "*I* seem to be able to separate them, to have the physical part without the other, and it leaves me feeling empty and used and worthless. I can't let that happen to me again."

"You're talking about with Gideon, right?" Jason looked at her intently.

"There hasn't been anyone else."

"I see," he said thoughtfully. "Well, it looks as if I've got my work cut out for me!"

"Whatever do you mean?" Vanessa stared at him.

"Well, someone has to prove to you that denying your sexuality isn't the answer," he said cheerfully, getting to his feet. "Come along now, I'll walk you to your car. Let's just go check on Emily first."

Vanessa followed him up to the fourth floor of the tall, narrow house. A night-light glowed softly in the large bedroom under the sloping eaves. Emily's discarded clothes were scattered over the thickly carpeted floor and Jason bent with a quick smile and a slight shake of his head to pick them up, folding them neatly before putting them on a chair.

"One of these days . . ." he whispered.

Vanessa smiled, leaning against the doorjamb, watching

as he approached the pretty, canopied bed.

Emily stirred as he drew the coverlet over her shoulders. Her eyes opened for an instant. "Daddy?"

"Yes, poppet." He dropped beside the bed, resting easily on his ankles. "I'm just going to walk Vanessa to her car. About ten minutes—you'll be okay?"

"'Course." The sleepy voice sounded slightly scornful. Jason dropped a light kiss on his daughter's smooth brow and got to his feet. Vanessa felt a curious pang as he crossed the room, soft-footed, toward her. That was a relationship she had not yet experienced, perhaps never would. She and Gideon had talked about having children once upon a time, but they'd both been students then, with too little money and too many books to pay for. Once those pressures had eased, their marriage had been on the skids—but at least they'd avoided the mistake of assuming that a child would heal all breaches!

They walked briskly through the cold, windy night. Vanessa unlocked the door of the Fiat and turned slowly toward Jason.

He smiled. "Let's revert to my original plan, shall we? Put your hands in your pockets and keep them there."

Vanessa sputtered softly, but did as he asked. He took her face between his hands and she could feel her eyes melting with her body under that sensuous, promising expression. "I don't think this is going to work," she muttered.

"It will, if you keep your hands away from me." He grinned. "Try for self-control rather than self-denial." Then his lips came down again, undemanding at first, close-mouthed, firm, warm. His tongue ran over her lips, pushed in light, darting movements between them until with a curious sigh she parted for him. He was inside her head it seemed, that muscular presence filling her being, not invading, not taking, just becoming a part of her.

"There now," he whispered, standing back slightly. "That wasn't so difficult, was it?"

"Yes, it was," she stated with a rueful grin.

Jason laughed outright, turned her around, and patted her bottom lightly. "Get in the car, firefly!"

"Hey, don't do that," she objected sharply.

"Why not?" he asked, holding the door open, laughing down at her as she settled herself behind the wheel. "I've been longing to ever since I first met you—you have an eminently pattable bottom."

"That is so sexist," she protested fiercely.

"I don't think it is," he remarked seriously, but his eyes were crinkling and dancing at her. "You can pat mine any time you like!"

"Oh, Jason!" Any further remark she might have made was prevented as he closed the door firmly, shutting out his laughter and leaving her with hers.

Chapter 5

VANESSA WALKED BRISKLY through the hallways of Carlysle Electronics on her way to her office. Her determinedly cheerful greetings to those she passed received grudging responses. It was tough being the most unpopular kid on the block, she reflected with a rueful grimace, but she was used to it. The first couple of weeks were always the worst.

In the two weeks since she'd started working here full-time, her efforts to establish a rapport with the staff had been generally blocked. She had sent out a confidential questionnaire asking for information on the jobs people were doing, whom they reported to, what complaints they might have, and any suggestions for improvement in their working conditions. The questionnaires were coming back to her very slowly, and only after considerable prompting, in spite of her reiterated assurances of the confidentiality of the information. An uneasy silence tended to fall when she walked into a room; alerting coughs were heard as she approached knots of previously animated employees.

She had quickly given up eating in the cafeteria—it was too uncomfortable to sit alone at a table for four surrounded by an all-too-obvious silence in the midst of vigorously chattering groups. Something was going to have to be done, and soon, if she was to succeed in cracking this particular nut. She needed the cooperation that only came with trust; the problem with Carlysle Electronics was that there was little trust at any level, and if one was tarred with the administration brush, none whatsoever.

She needed Jason's help badly, but he seemed to spend so much time flitting around the country overseeing his other plants that he had little time to spare for this one. Vanessa had an uneasy feeling that he expected her to wave a magic wand and solve all his problems in one fell swoop. Unfortunately, since he was, by default at least, responsible for those very problems, he had to become more actively involved in their solution. Her most urgent task, she decided as she reached her office, was to convince him of this fact. Once he returned from Dallas, that was.

She nudged the door of her office with her hip, her hands fully occupied with the cup of canteen sludge that went by the name of coffee, and the thick ring-binder that never left her side unless it was safely locked in the file cabinet. The intercom buzzed as she dumped everything on her desk.

"Hello," she responded brightly.

"Dr. Harrington," Mrs. Macy's voice drifted down the wire, "Mr. Carlysle would like to see you in his office right away."

Vanessa frowned. So he was back, was he? Obviously, his role as big boss was going to his head.

"I can't leave my desk right now, Mrs. Macy," she said politely. "I'm expecting an important call. If it's really urgent, perhaps Mr. Carlysle would like to join me in my office. Otherwise, I'll come up this afternoon."

"I'll give him your message," the disembodied voice declared, and Vanessa replaced the receiver. Something must be bothering Jason; that peremptory summons was not his usual style——at least not with her. She turned back to the stack of papers on her desk, and quickly became immersed in her work.

Jason followed his brisk knock on her door immediately, almost before she had had time to register the disturbance.

"Hi there." She smiled, her heart somersaulting again at

the sight of that tall, broad-shouldered figure. "How was Dallas?"

"Hard work," was the brief response. "Just what do you mean by sending me supercilious messages via my secretary?" He was holding a sheaf of papers and looking distinctly annoyed as he perched himself on the windowsill.

"You're a fine one to talk!" Vanessa rose instantly to the attack, the light of battle shining in her eyes. "I am not, thank heavens, an employee of this company. In fact, not to put too fine a point on it, I'm surprised you've got any employees at all! I will not be informed that 'Mr. Carlysle wants to see me in his office immediately'—"

"I didn't say that," Jason interrupted quietly, but she continued, unheeding.

"If you have something to say to me, you could surely do me the courtesy of calling me yourself, or at least *asking* me to come see you? I work here purely on a consulting basis and—"

"Vanessa, would you back up a minute? We appear to have some crossed wires here, and if you continue in that vein they're going to get impossibly tangled!" His voice cut sharply across her impassioned speech and she took a deep breath.

"What do you mean?"

"I mean, firefly, that whatever message you appear to have received was not the one I sent. I would have called you myself, but I was expecting a conference call and merely asked Mrs. Macy to find out if you could spare a few minutes—at your convenience!"

"Oh," Vanessa said thoughtfully. "What message did you get from me?"

"That you were far too busy to come upstairs and would be prepared to see me in *your* office."

"I didn't say exactly that." She frowned reflectively. "I think I know what's going on."

"Well, I wish I did," Jason snapped with unusual irritability.

"Mrs. Macy's playing games," Vanessa stated flatly. "It's not unusual. She's actually trying to set up a dogfight, with you and me as the antagonists." She shrugged casually. "Not to worry—we'll just have to be on the watch for it, that's all."

Jason got off the windowsill and began pacing around the small space. "Look, Vanessa, I don't know how to say this, but, quite frankly, this place is now even a worse mess than when you came on the scene. Everyone's in an uproar. Look at these." He held out the sheaf of papers toward her. "There's an ultimatum from the union in there, two petitions from various departments, and Mallon's resignation—all due to your presence."

Vanessa said nothing, concentrating instead on reading through the material he'd handed her. "No real problem," she pronounced eventually. "They're confused about my role, that's all. But you should accept Mallon's resignation."

"What! Vanessa, you've got a screw loose! The man's been with the company for thirty years," Jason exclaimed incredulously.

"Sure he has," she replied soothingly. "That is why, so long as you make it clear that you accept his resignation reluctantly and give him a face-saving out, he'll withdraw it."

"I thought you operated on very liberal principles when it came to worker/management relationships?" He shook his head in puzzlement.

"I do," Vanessa replied cheerfully. "But before you can become liberal you have to have trust and respect. As far as the employees of this company are concerned, the administration operates on whim and favoritism and as a result they're entitled to milk the system for all it's worth. Now, Jack Mallon reckons that for the last thirty years he's done his own thing. He's a poor manager, by the way," she added as afterthought, "he hasn't had enough incentive to become otherwise. So, you try to threaten that comfortable carelessness of his, and he's going to kick. He doesn't know where he stands right now, none of them do. You have to start with Jack—tell him firmly that there are going to be changes, you'd like him to be a part of them but if he can't see his way to becoming so, then, of course, you understand."

"Look, Vanessa, I'm not saying you don't know your job—"

"I should hope not!" she interrupted his hesitant beginning.

Jason sighed and tried again. "You have to admit that the situation is worse now than it was before."

"Wounds need to bleed before they heal," Vanessa stated firmly. "I know exactly what I'm doing and exactly what's going on. It's part of a process, that's all."

"I don't like it." Jason stopped pacing and looked at her closely.

"Are you telling me you want to call it off?" Vanessa asked directly.

"Yes."

The short affirmative hung in the air. She fiddled with the top of her fountain pen, unconsciously wrinkling her nose as she thought.

"I'm sorry, firefly."

"Don't call me that right now!" she expostulated. "It's not appropriate, and I'm thinking."

"Sorry, Dr. Harrington." He gave a small apologetic bow. "But what's there to think about?"

"I have to find the right words to convince you you're wrong." She looked up with sudden decision. "Okay, Jason—we've set a process in motion and so far have done nothing more than tear down some walls, leaving very ragged foundations. If I leave now without putting the pieces together again, you really will be worse off than you were before." He remained silent and she continued swiftly, "I have a suggestion."

Jason grinned slowly. "Surprise, surprise! Fire away, then."

"I'd like you to call a meeting of all staff, in working hours so they don't feel it's an imposition. Imply that attendance is compulsory, but don't enforce it—you won't need to, anyway. No one's going to miss this," Vanessa added with a quick grin, beginning to scribble rapidly on the legal pad in front of her. "Something along these lines." She handed the pad across to him.

Jason read it through, frowning deeply, then shook his head decisively. "No. Sorry, Vanessa, but this really won't work."

"What do you mean, it won't work?" she overrode with ill-concealed irritation. "I just want to make a presentation to the entire staff, explaining what's going on and what we hope to achieve. This way, it'll prevent mixed messages and crossed wires. If everyone hears what I have to say—"

"I said no!"

It was his "Emily" voice, and Vanessa's hackles rose. "I heard you the first time," she said coldly. "You might do me the courtesy of letting me finish."

"Look, we're not getting anywhere, Vanessa." Jason spoke with an obvious effort to sound reasonable. "You're suggesting that you try single-handedly to persuade the staff to cooperate in your endeavors and then you will continue or not on the basis of their decision. They vote on whether or not they want you around. Is that correct?"

"Perfectly," she said quietly.

"That is my decision, not theirs," he declared emphatically.

"That attitude, Jason, is going to leave you up the creek without a paddle!"

"They'll tear you to pieces," he stated flatly.

Vanessa chuckled softly. "That's how much you know. I am more than capable of dealing with such situations— I've done it many times. Relax, Jason. I can look after myself."

"I'm not saying you can't." Jason ran an exasperated hand through his hair, causing it to stand out in a wiry halo around his head. "I just don't like it."

"Look, I do *not* need protecting." Vanessa stood up, irritation at his obstinacy beginning to get the better of her. "This habit you have of continually mopping me up and dusting me off and generally directing things has got to stop! Do I make myself clear?"

"Don't talk to me like that, Vanessa. I'm not Gideon," he said quietly, the tightness of his lips and the stillness of his body the only signs of the control he was exercising.

"No, and if you were, the last thing I'd have to worry about would be overprotectiveness," she snapped. "You're running scared, but I don't happen to be a coward—I like to finish what I've started, however unpleasant it may be!"

They stood facing each other across the small office like a pair of angry dogs preparing for battle.

"You're one of the few people who can make me angry, Vanessa. I am not going to continue this now." He turned on his heel and marched out of the room, shutting the door very quietly behind him.

Vanessa stood glaring at the door. Typical male response—I don't like what you're saying, so I won't stay and listen. With a frustrated shake of her head, she returned to her desk. No point now in continuing with her analysis. How she hated leaving things in the middle! In total exasperation, she began to order and tidy the papers—they'd have to be shredded, but Jason could do that for himself. It wasn't her responsibility any longer; let him make sure that they didn't fall into the wrong hands.

The job took her longer than she'd expected, mainly because in the process of sorting she found herself involuntarily analyzing, picking up threads she hadn't noticed before, becoming totally absorbed again in the problems of Carlysle Electronics.

At last, however, everything was in order, and with angry disappointment in her soul she stalked upstairs to Jason's office. Mrs. Macy gave her a slightly anxious look as she walked in and asked testily, "Is Mr. Carlysle free?"

"He's on the phone right now, Dr. Harrington, but no one's with him," the secretary replied.

Reflecting that since they had nothing to talk about, Jason's being on the phone wouldn't matter, Vanessa rapped briskly on his door and went in.

Jason looked up, startled, and waved her toward a chair, but she shook her head briefly and dumped the stack of papers under his nose, saying curtly, "You'll need to shred them, but you might as well see what you paid for."

Jason put his hand over the mouthpiece. "Just hold on a minute, would you? I'll be through here in just a second."

"There's nothing to hold on for," she responded tartly and turned toward the door, ignoring his imperative "Vanessa!"

Back in her office, she checked quickly through her desk to make sure nothing was left behind, picked up her purse and coat, and headed for the door. The intercom buzzed and she hesitated, but only momentarily, before closing the door behind her with decisive finality.

She drove unhappily to her own office, glad that Hilary had the day off so she wouldn't be required to produce either explanations or small talk. It took her an hour to respond to the calls and messages on the answering machine, and some of her irritability vanished under the anodyne of work. Until the phone rang, and Jason's voice broke, without preamble, into her fragile equilibrium.

"Firefly, what the hell's going on here?"

"Mr. Carlysle," she said icily, "you may call me Vanessa or Dr. Harrington. If you have any questions about the material I left you, I'll be very happy to answer them. Otherwise, I am very busy right now."

"Vanessa, would you please stop behaving like this!"

"I am not behaving like anything," she snapped. "Now, you'll have to excuse me. There's a call on the other line and Hilary isn't in today. Good-bye." She put the phone down with a thump and chewed her lip crossly. She really wasn't behaving very well, but she just didn't feel able to talk to Jason at the moment. Tomorrow, when the sharp edge of disappointment had blunted, she would write him a polite, formal letter bringing everything to a businesslike close.

The drive home seemed worse than usual that evening— the commuter traffic heavier, slower, and more incompetent than ever.

"I'm so miserable, Jilly," she greeted her friend bluntly as she stalked into the living room and flung herself down on the couch. "Fill me with gin, there's a love."

Jilly looked at her with concern. "What's up?"

"Jason's decided to cancel the program, just because of a few perfectly normal wrinkles." She ran her hands despondently through her hair, pulling out the pins to release the neat topknot. "And now I've behaved abominably. I'll have to write and apologize. I ought to call him, of course, but I can't talk to him right now—I'll only be rude again."

Jilly whistled soundlessly as she handed her a tall glass frosted with condensation. "Don't tell me you did a 'Gideon' on him?"

"Sort of," Vanessa confessed miserably. "I can't stand it when people won't listen to me. It's my job to deal with these things and I know exactly how to go about it. He was being thoroughly obstinate and blind—but that was no excuse for my rudeness," she added with a heavy sigh, taking a long, refreshing sip of her drink.

"He didn't sound particularly annoyed when he called." Jilly hitched her long legs over the arm of her chair and observed Vanessa over the rim of her glass.

Vanessa's heart lurched. "When did he call?" she asked carefully.

"You mean the first time or the third?" Jilly grinned mischievously.

"Stop teasing, Jilly. What did he say?"

"He wants you to call him at home. As I said, he didn't sound particularly annoyed, just rather purposeful." Jilly examined the contents of her glass with great deliberation.

"Oh." Vanessa frowned. "Well, I don't think I will, actually. I'd rather deal with this on paper. It's a business affair, not personal."

Jilly looked at her skeptically. "Whatever you say, Van. But if you ask me, that clear head of yours has become a little muddled recently."

Vanessa sucked in her lower lip on a sharp inhalation, but her innate honesty forced her to say quietly, "You may well be right. There's something about Jason that's . . . oh, I don't know . . . sort of eating into me. It's not just the chemical attraction"—she gave a quick grin—"although that's powerful enough! But he's so calm and determined.

Sometimes I feel he could be my 'port in a storm'—if you'll excuse the cliché."

Jilly nodded gravely. "You've spent a long time battling the ocean waves alone, Van. Maybe you should consider dropping anchor for a while. It's not that dangerous, you know."

"Isn't it?" Vanessa asked softly. "I've tried it once, remember? The anchor didn't hold that time."

Jilly stood up briskly. "Gideon wasn't right for you, nor you for him. He needs a soft little kitten for a wife—someone to have his slippers and his dinner waiting for him when he comes home. Not a woman who's more than capable of competing with him on every level and, if put to the test, would generally win. Your problem, Van, is that you see everything in terms of your own failure—if things don't work out, it's all your fault. You have to learn to share responsibility a bit—give yourself a break once in a while, kid!" She moved decisively toward the door. "I'm going out with Tom tonight—I've done enough lecturing for one day. Have a good evening!" With a cheery wave, she closed the living room door firmly.

A minute later, Vanessa heard the front door click and rose wearily from the couch. No-nonsense Jilly had, as usual, turned her sharp, practical lawyer's eyes in the right direction. A hot shower was the answer right now. She had to clear her mind of today's upheaval before she could plan a new course of action.

The scalding water did its work. Once, she heard the phone ring, pathetically insistent through the noisy cascade, but she checked an automatic response to run dripping to catch it. If it was Jason, she wasn't ready to talk just yet, and anyone else would call again.

Pulling on a pair of old jeans and a sweater, she wandered into the kitchen in search of dinner.

The front doorbell made her jump as she was hovering indecisively between the unexciting choice of canned soup or an egg. She and Jilly really had to get their housekeeping organized a bit more efficiently! The bell rang again, impatiently, and with a resigned sigh she went to answer it.

"Oh, it's you," she stated rather ungraciously as she looked into the slate-colored eyes of Jason Carlysle.

Jason looked down the hallway with a considering frown. "That seems like a fairly accurate observation." He brought his hand from behind his back with a courtly flourish, presenting her with an enormous, exquisite bouquet of long-stemmed American Beauties.

"Ah," Vanessa breathed, totally taken aback by the unexpectedness of the gift. What an extraordinarily unpredictable man he was! Her behavior today, in spite of a fair degree of provocation, merited a show of annoyance, and instead she received a present.

"Thank you. They're lovely." She stood holding the flowers, completely at a loss.

"You know, I've been thinking all day you need to take a lesson in manners, Vanessa, but this is ridiculous. Are you going to keep me standing in the hallway all evening?"

Vanessa flushed. Stepping backward, she pulled the door wide, still unable to think of anything suitable to say. Jason strode past her with a courteous smile of thanks, preceding her into the living room as she gestured in vague invitation.

She found her voice at last. "Can I get you a drink?"

"Scotch and water, please." He sat on the couch, an expression of total ease and relaxation on his craggy face.

He was wearing the most superb suit, she noticed almost absently—charcoal gray with a glimmering white shirt and a silky, rose-colored tie. Vanessa felt distinctly scruffy with her unmade-up face and hair tucked carelessly behind her ears.

"Thanks." He took the glass from her, and sipped carefully before continuing briskly, "Now, why don't we clear the air with an exchange of apologies?"

Vanessa took a deep breath, turning to arrange the roses in a blue Wedgwood vase. "I suppose I did overreact a little," she conceded finally.

"Is that the best you can do?" The incredulous exclamation was accompanied by a pair of eyebrows disappearing into his scalp.

"All right." Vanessa turned back to face him. "I'm sorry

I yelled at you and I'm sorry I called you a coward, but you really made me furious, Jason! I've been in this business for a long time now, and I don't need the protection of a male umbrella. I know exactly what I can handle and what I can't."

Jason said nothing, just continued to regard her thoughtfully as if he were still waiting for something.

She chewed her lip and sighed heavily. "I'm sorry I stomped off like that."

Jason smiled suddenly. "That was like getting blood out of a stone! All right, my turn now. I apologize for doubting you, Vanessa, and I'm sorry I sounded a trifle autocratic."

"A trifle!" she exclaimed, then fell silent as he shook his head quickly, continuing, "You are quite right, it's far too early to 'run scared,' as you put it. I've set up that meeting for you for the day after tomorrow, at ten o'clock. All right?"

Vanessa nodded. "Yes, that'll be good. Why the change of heart?"

"I accepted Jack Mallon's resignation," he said briefly.

"And?" Vanessa prompted.

"He behaved exactly as you said. I also put Mrs. Macy straight on a few things," he added with a twisted grin. "How long is it going to go on like this, Vanessa? I'm a very mild, generally conciliatory man, and this out-of-character behavior is getting to be a real strain."

Vanessa laughed suddenly. "Don't give me that, Jason Carlysle. You're as tough as nails under that smooth exterior. Anyway, don't worry. If the vote goes against me, I'll get out of your hair for good, and without another fight!"

"Then I'm just going to have to hope it doesn't, aren't I?" he murmured, his eyes taking on a smoky intensity again. She knew that her response to that look was nakedly revealed in her face, and she turned hastily, beginning to fuss with the roses again.

"Go get changed, firefly," he said quietly. "We're running late."

"Running late for what?" She whirled around in surprise.

"The National Symphony Orchestra at the Kennedy Center, then dinner," he replied blandly.

"Are you asking me for a date?"

"It certainly looks that way." He grinned. "Although I'm not exactly asking."

Vanessa decided to ignore the provocation. "Does that mean another good-night kiss?" she inquired.

He nodded firmly.

"Nothing more, though—agreed?"

"Vanessa, I've already told you—*you* are going to be doing the asking next time. You won't meet with any obstacles, though, I assure you." He smiled. "You have about ten minutes to get ready. You look remarkably well scrubbed. I assume you were in the shower when I last called?"

Vanessa had the grace to blush. "I'll be as quick as I can," she muttered and whisked herself out of the room.

They parked under the elegant pillared building of the Kennedy Center and rode the escalators to the Grand Foyer. "We have time for a glass of champagne," Jason announced cheerfully, easing her with a light arm on her shoulder over to the bar.

"Let's go on the terrace." Vanessa took the small glass of bubbly liquid with a smile of thanks and they pushed through the heavy glass doors into the chill evening air on the broad terrace overlooking the river. "Building this place was a real inspiration." She took a deep breath, feeling the river breeze lift her hair away from her face. "I always drink a toast to J.F.K. when I'm here."

Jason laughed softly, and touched her glass with his before sipping. "I do love the way you're so enthusiastic about everything. You even wade into battle with your eyes shining."

Vanessa tucked a strand of hair behind one ear. "Yes, well, perhaps we shouldn't talk about battles right now. I don't feel remotely combative."

"That's good, it makes a nice change," Jason said gravely. "Let's go listen to some Beethoven."

In the silken luxury of Maison Blanche after the concert, Vanessa examined her menu, a slight smile curving her lips.

Jason looked up instantly from his own study. He was

the most responsive man, she thought, as he asked, "What's funny?"

"I was just wondering what you'd say if I offered to split the check," she said playfully.

"Use your imagination!"

"I just did." She laughed. "Which is why I wasn't going to offer."

He smiled. "What do you want to eat?" he asked, resting his elbows on the table, his chin in the palm of his hand as he examined her with that close, all-seeing intensity. His crisp white shirt cuffs with their dull gold cuff links glistened under the soft candlelight. Her eyes became fixed on the heavy gold signet ring on his right hand, the smooth, neat fingernails, the rather knobbly knuckles on the long fingers. He had large hands; in fact, he was a large man altogether, she reflected. Jilly was right—he was quite the sexiest, most attractive man she'd ever spent time with. Judging by the covert glances he was getting from their female neighbors, she wasn't the only one who thought so.

"Firefly?"

"I'm sorry—I was miles away." She gave a quick, guilty shake of her head. "What did you say?"

"I asked you what you'd like to eat." His eyes danced again. You, she thought distractedly, and I will, if you go on looking at me like that.

"Vanessa, what *is* the matter?" He was laughing openly now, but with a degree of puzzlement.

"Nothing's the matter." She pulled herself together with a supreme effort. "I can't decide what I want—I feel wishy-washy this evening."

"I won't argue with that. But if you can't decide, you'll have to let me do it for you."

"Okay," she agreed cheerfully, closing her menu with a decisive snap. "Let's see what you come up with."

Jason pursed his mouth, sucking in his cheeks as he continued to examine her. "Oysters," he said firmly.

Vanessa grinned slightly. "They're supposed to be an aphrodisiac."

"Do you need one?" he murmured softly. A deeply sensuous smile was on his lips and in his eyes again, and her skin prickled.

"Change the subject, please."

"You brought it up," he reminded her.

"Yes, I know. It just slipped out. I'm sorry."

"Don't apologize." He turned back to his menu. "I think we'll follow the oysters with the *carré d'agneau*. Let's see what we should drink with it."

The large silver platter arrived and was placed ceremoniously in the middle of the table between them. Vanessa licked her lips in anticipation. There was something about those rough gray shells with their succulent burdens resting on cracked ice, interspersed with the deep yellow of sliced lemon, that appealed visually almost more than it did gastronomically. The first slightly fishy, slightly sea-tasting morsel slipped down her throat.

"Jason," she began, wondering why she was about to ask this, "since your divorce, have you had any . . . I mean many . . ." It wasn't coming out right! "Sorry, forget I spoke."

"Why?" He frowned. "I can't imagine why you're having such difficulty asking a perfectly simple question."

"I suppose because it seems a rather impertinent question and I can't imagine why I want to know, anyway," she explained hesitantly.

"Well, I'll tell you this much—celibacy has never been my long suit," he stated matter-of-factly.

Vanessa gave a wry chuckle. "I didn't imagine it was— I really can't see you in a hair shirt in a monastery!"

"Any more than I can imagine you in this self-imposed nunnery of yours," he replied evenly.

"We were talking about you," Vanessa stated quietly. "Don't answer this if you'd rather not, but have you had any serious affairs since your divorce?"

"A couple." Silence fell for a moment as Vanessa wondered if she had offended him by the question. "At the moment, however, all my energies seem to be going into a long and immensely frustrating pursuit of a tempestuous firefly." The sudden statement brought her head up sharply.

"Why don't you just give up, then?" she asked with genuine curiosity.

"I'm a very determined man," he observed tranquilly. "Also excessively easygoing and reasonable. I could give up, or I could push you." A suggestive note suddenly crept into his voice. "If I did the latter, I suspect I wouldn't have to push too hard, but I prefer to wait for you to come to me."

Vanessa couldn't deny his statement and didn't attempt to as she reached absently toward the platter.

"Hey, I'm not *that* reasonable!" Jason suddenly leaned forward, tapping her wrist smartly with his fork. "You've had your six—that last oyster's mine!"

"Oh, sorry, I wasn't counting." She withdrew her hand hastily.

"Fibber!" He laughed. "You were hoping to sneak in and gobble it up before I'd noticed."

Vanessa laughed with him, and the tension of the last few minutes was broken as by unspoken mutual consent they reverted to neutral subjects.

This time she didn't protest as Jason walked her to her door. "Would you like to come in for a nightcap?" She felt for her key in her purse.

Jason shook his head. "No, thanks. It's late and I'm taking the early shuttle to New York tomorrow."

"So you won't be in the office all day?" Vanessa was conscious only of disappointment.

"No, but I'll be there the day after, for the meeting."

"Look, Jason," she said firmly. "Maybe it would be best if you weren't there, if you're really uncomfortable about the operation."

"That, Vanessa, is a suggestion I prefer to ignore." His tone was level and quiet, but she'd have had to be blind and deaf to have missed the message.

"As you wish." She shrugged. "I'll see you on Wednesday, then. Thank you for a lovely evening." Why did she feel so ridiculously nervous—like a teenager on her first date?

A finger lightly tipped her chin, warm lips lightly touched the tip of her nose. "Thank you for coming, Vanessa. Good night." He was walking away from her down the hallway. Vanessa felt a silly urge to stick her tongue out at that broad, retreating back. He was so confusingly unpredictable. However, in all honesty, she admitted reluctantly as she let herself into the darkened hallway, she was getting no more than her just desserts. She had no right to complain if he decided not to give her the promised good-night kiss.

Chapter 6

IT WAS SIX o'clock the following evening before Vanessa
finally started putting together the presentation for the next
day's meeting. She'd had a totally frustrating day, starting
with a flat tire on her way to her own office, followed by
Hilary's absence with a sick child and a succession of com-
plications with the Patterson contract that she'd thought
she'd dealt with earlier. She'd arrived at Carlysle Electronics
in the early evening instead of midday, as she had intended,
and had a good six hours of work ahead of her to produce
the presentation tomorrow. And she knew that it had to be
good—indeed, better than good—if she was to win over
this particular, very hostile group.

The night seemed to vanish as she sorted through slides,
charts, questionnaires. She wrote up a couple of typical
situations illustrating the benefits of an employee-assistance
program. There was a mountain of material to photocopy,
and wearily she trudged down the hallway to the copying
room. Her eyes began to glaze under the unending stream
of neatly printed white paper sliding into the tray to be
collected, ordered, and stapled. If she had been able to get
the material prepared in the daytime, this boring, automatic
task could have been done by someone else.

"What the devil are you doing? Do you know what time
it is?"

She spun around from the long table now heaped with

orderly piles of paper. Jason was standing in the doorway, his briefcase under one arm, a brown bag in his other hand, and an expression of total incredulity on his face.

"No, I don't, actually." She answered his last question first.

"It's six o'clock in the morning!"

"Well, what are *you* doing here?" Attack seemed the best form of defense at this point.

"I often come in at this time," he replied impatiently. "I can get a lot of work done before the phones start ringing and the place fills up. That, however, does *not* explain what you're doing here!"

"Maybe my reasons are the same as yours," she prevaricated, wondering why she couldn't just tell him to mind his own business.

Jason strode purposefully across the room toward her. She was backed up against the table and faced his scrutiny with curious, incomprehensible defiance.

"You've been here all night, haven't you?" he demanded.

"Well, what's it to you if I have?" she muttered, feeling ridiculously like a guilty child caught with her hand in the cookie jar.

"You idiot, Vanessa!" He put his burdens down on the table and, taking her shoulders, gave her a slight, exasperated shake. "What sort of nonsense *is* this?"

"Don't you talk to me like that, Jason Carlysle. I'm not Emily," she protested hotly.

"No, more's the pity," he replied grimly. "If you were I'd know exactly how to deal with you!"

"Oh, and how would that be—pray?" Her chin jutted dangerously as fatigue receded in the face of annoyance.

Jason took her chin firmly between thumb and forefinger, his grip only tightening as she tried to pull away. "I'd send you to bed without any supper!" Suddenly, his lips twitched. "Actually, that's not a bad idea, but in your case it would be without any loving."

Vanessa's anger disappeared under the now laughing eyes. "Don't be ridiculous, Jason," she protested and then sniffed hungrily. "Is that coffee you've got in there?"

He released her and handed over the brown bag. "Take it up to my office and I'll go get some more."

Vanessa peered inside. "There's food in here," she muttered, breathing deeply. "Real food—not some dreary muffin—isn't there?"

Jason gave a shout of laughter. "Grilled cheese and bacon—the only breakfast worth eating, in my opinion."

"Did you hold the pickle?" she questioned eagerly, her own eyes dancing.

"Of course!" he declared.

"You're a man after my own heart."

"Well, take it upstairs and I'll repeat the order." Powerful hands turned her toward the door.

"I just want to finish up here first."

"You will do exactly as you are told, Vanessa, for probably the first time in your relatively short life!"

"Hey, stop playing macho man," she protested, but was unable to prevent her laughter. "You're not very good at it, you know."

"I can learn—now, march!" He pushed her ahead of him out the door and she went relatively willingly, clutching the brown bag. There was very little left to do and a short break wouldn't come amiss.

When Jason joined her upstairs she was licking her fingers slowly, having devoured the sandwich in double-quick time.

"I got you more coffee." He handed her another cup. "Now, could you explain just what lay behind this piece of craziness?" He unwrapped his own sandwich, taking a large bite with a sigh of satisfaction.

"It was not craziness. I had to put together today's presentation and didn't have time yesterday."

"But how can you possibly expect to perform in front of that audience red-eyed and white-faced, with your mind all jumbled and your words lost in a series of yawns?" he pointed out.

"I'll go home, take a shower, change, and be as good as new," she responded confidently. Then she added with an anxious frown, "Do I really look that awful?"

"I was being kind," Jason said bluntly. "I have a much better suggestion."

"Oh?" She looked at him cautiously.

"You take a nap on the couch until nine-thirty." He glanced at his watch. "That gives you three hours. Then you can shower here, have a second breakfast, and you just might feel borderline human again."

"I have to change my clothes, so I must go home."

"Is Jilly there?"

"Yes, but what's that got to do with anything?" Vanessa frowned.

"Simple. I'll send a messenger to pick up some fresh clothes and anything else you need. I'm sure Jilly will put some things together for you. I'll phone her about it later. Jason sounded so calm, so logical, so reasonable, that her objections began to fade.

"Oh." That seemed to be that—one last try, though. "It's going to look very odd to Mrs. Macy to see me asleep on your couch."

"Why don't you let me deal with Mrs. Macy? I'm getting much better at it just recently." Jason wiped his fingers vigorously and looked at her. "Now, firefly, enough objections—get your head down; you're just wasting precious sleeping time."

Vanessa shrugged and went toward the couch. "Oh, I forgot," she said suddenly.

"Now what?"

"I left all that stuff in the copying room. I haven't quite finished stapling the last sheets."

"Someone else can do that," came the calm response.

He was right, of course. With a sigh, she curled up on the couch, pulling a cushion under her head, and was instantly asleep.

"Wake up, sleepyhead." The soft, insistent voice accompanied the light but firm shake that brought her slowly, reluctantly into dazed, eye-blinking awareness.

"Oh, Lord!" she groaned. "I'd have done better to have stayed awake. I feel awful."

"You'll feel better in a while. Try this." Jason was resting on his heels beside the couch, smiling at her as he pressed a steaming cup of coffee into her enfeebled hands. Even through her sleep-misted eyes, she could read the soft, tender message in that smile; heat crept slowly up her body, starting with her curled toes. Not even Gideon in his heyday had looked at her quite like that.

"Did you get hold of Jilly?" Hastily, she struggled into a sitting position, cupping her hands around the mug.

"Yes. Your clothes are over there." Jason pointed toward a small suitcase, still not getting to his feet.

"What did she say?" Vanessa took a deep gulp and shuddered with pleasure as the very strong coffee hit her solar plexus.

"We had a very pleasant chat." He grinned. "She had some choice remarks to make about stubborn, single-minded workaholics—I haven't been so completely in agreement with anyone in a long time!" He rose to his feet easily, striding long-legged across the room to answer the imperative ring of the phone.

Vanessa made a face—she should have expected as much. Jilly never pulled her punches, and neither, it seemed, did Jason Carlysle. With a strong-minded effort, she swung her feet to the floor, picked up the suitcase, and disappeared into the bathroom. She blessed Jilly silently—her friend had forgotten nothing, not even deodorant, toothbrush, and toothpaste.

She was brushing her teeth vigorously when there was a sharp rap at the door. "Yes?" she mumbled through a mouthful of foam. The door opened and Jason stuck his head around.

"Do you want more breakfast..." His voice died as his eyes took in her body, scantily clad in bra and bikini pants, bent over the basin. "Sorry." He sighed. "I thought you said 'come in.'" He retreated, closing the door quietly behind him.

Vanessa spat toothpaste under the running tap with unnecessary vigor. She wasn't exactly embarrassed—she wore less on the beach most of the summer and thought nothing of it. But in present circumstances...She shrugged and pushed her nose around the door. "I could use a dreary muffin and more coffee, please."

"Coming up," the cheery voice reassured her, and she retired again behind the closed door.

A rust-colored suede skirt, matching vest, and tawny-brown silk shirt was exactly right. Her face was pale, dark smudges under the eyes, but that was no problem. If she looked a little tired, she'd get more sympathy than with a bright, bouncy, excessive confidence. She applied the lightest of makeup, and brushed her heavy red-gold hair vigorously. Up or down? Vanessa frowned. Down—a little calculated vulnerability would do no harm. Rolling her discarded clothing into a heap, she pushed everything into the suitcase, tidied the small bathroom with swift efficiency, and emerged into the sun-filled office.

"One dreary muffin and as much coffee as you can handle, Dr. Harrington." Jason got up from the desk, poured coffee, and handed her a cup and a plate. "You really do know what you're doing, firefly," he murmured appreciatively. "You look fantastic—slightly ethereal, a little drawn and weary, and utterly businesslike."

Vanessa gave a small laugh. "I have to thank Jilly for her choice of clothes—I couldn't have done better myself."

The canteen was packed with curious, speculative, and distinctly hostile eyes. Vanessa's pulse rate was definitely faster than usual as she gave soft-voiced instructions about the placing of projector and screen, moved quietly down the expectant rows handing out the printed material. She kept a practiced smile on her face, and addressed the employees she knew by name. Jason was moving easily around the room, exchanging greetings, asking and answering the overly polite social questions that always went with sessions of this kind. Vanessa hadn't asked him to do this, had rather expected that he would sit in an uncomfortable, stony silence on the dais, but he had surprised her again and was doing the best softening-up job he could in the circumstances.

At last, judging that all was in order, she took her place behind the projector. Stage fright disappeared as she began to talk—this was the kind of challenge that set the adrenaline pumping and brought a sparkle to her green eyes.

Illustrating her points with visual aids, she began with a brief history of the development of employee-assistance programs and the philosophy that lay behind them. The point she most wanted to get across to this crowded room was the objective nature of the program, the fact that it was in no way to be seen as the long arm of management. From there, it was easy to explain her own job as an outside consultant, *not* a management spy, and to explain why she needed the information she had asked for and to what purpose it would be put. A ripple of interest ran through the room as, with the enthusiasm this always engendered in her, she explained her firm belief that all members of staff should be involved in the making of decisions that directly affected them, that they were the people best qualified to say what changes were needed and how to implement them.

She turned slightly toward Jason, sitting seemingly relaxed at the small table behind her, although his gaze had never once left the faces in the packed room as he assessed his employees' reactions.

"Mr. Carlysle has employed me to analyze the problems in this company, to find out what you would like done about them, and to prepare a program tailored to *your* needs," she finished quietly.

All eyes turned to Jason's still figure and he smiled slightly but said nothing, merely nodded his head in silent agreement.

"Okay now, any questions?" Vanessa perched herself on the corner of the table and looked out over the throng. Much of the hostility had disappeared, but there was still wariness.

"Yes." Al Green, the combative, domineering union head, got ponderously to his feet. Vanessa felt Jason stiffening behind her and made a small, reassuring gesture with her hand as it rested on the table supporting her weight.

"You're a very convincing lady," the large man declared. "But this all sounds too good to me—here you are telling us what a wonderful thing you're doing for everyone, how we'll be much happier, smiling and laughing as we work, loving every minute of it." A rumble of laughter ran through the room at the heavy sarcasm in his voice. "What I want to know is, what's the management going to get out of this?" He gave a short, satisfied nod and remained, challenging her, on his feet.

"Increased production, Mr. Green," Vanessa replied calmly.

"What did I tell you?" He turned toward the room. "This is some management con, just like all the others. Before you know it, they'll have us working to increased targets, fewer breaks—"

"Hold it, Mr. Green." Vanessa's voice, still evenly and quietly pitched, nevertheless stopped him in midtrack. "This is a very expensive program. You don't seriously expect management to invest in it without expecting something back? I never said the motives were purely altruistic."

"So you're not denying it, then?" A note of uncertainty crept into the booming, triumphant voice.

"I'd be very stupid to do so," she responded quietly. "Of course the object is higher production targets, less absenteeism, less goofing off, if you like." Ignoring his angry scowl at her blunt choice of words, she continued, "People work better voluntarily when they're happy with their working environment. All right, I'm not promising to turn you into the seven dwarfs, 'singing while you work.'" A ripple of laughter ran through the room. "But I am saying that if you choose to take advantage of the program, life around here could improve. And, quite frankly, from what I've seen in the last two weeks, it could use some improvement." It was a hard-hitting statement and produced a tense silence, some awkward shuffling, and some creaking of the hard canteen chairs.

"What do you mean, 'if we choose to take advantage of it'?" he demanded.

"You vote for me or against me," she said simply. "I'll abide by your decision."

"And what does Mr. Carlysle say to that?"

Jason spoke up softly. "Mr. Carlysle, Al, says he's not prepared to fight Dr. Harrington. He doesn't think he'd win."

Even Al Green joined in the laughter this time. "So it's really up to us?" he questioned again.

"Absolutely," Vanessa stated positively. "Do you want a secret ballot or a show of hands?"

Al frowned. "Show of hands will do," he pronounced eventually, coming up to the dais, taking charge of the meeting. "Raise your hand if she stays," he commanded.

Vanessa held herself still, presenting a cool exterior as she watched hands rise, at first hesitantly and then with increased assurance as people glanced at their neighbors, muttered to each other. It looked like more than half the room.

"Those against." There were quite a few of them. Jack Mallon's hand was firmly raised, as were a significant number of other middle-management hands. The vote was in her favor, but the battle far from won. Vanessa was under no illusions on that score.

"Looks like you stay, Dr. Harrington," Al announced.

Vanessa contented herself with a brief nod and the smallest smile, beginning to gather up her papers as the meeting broke up. Jason remained sitting at the table until the room emptied.

"That was some performance," he remarked into the sudden hush.

"It was just a beginning," Vanessa responded shortly. "Don't imagine for one moment that this has put an end to the opposition. I rather suspect there's going to be some dirty undercover fighting in the next few weeks."

"I'm sure you'll be able to handle it," he stated firmly. "You're even tougher than I thought."

"Is that a compliment?" She turned to look at him, feeling suddenly overwhelmingly tired now that the excitement was over and her sleepless night was beginning to catch up with her.

"Yes, I think so," he said with a considering smile. "But tough or no, I'd like you to go home to bed now."

"You're ordering me around again." Vanessa attempted to glare at him, but succeeded only in yawning deeply.

"Oh, I wouldn't say that." He grinned. "But I will say

that if you're not tucked up in bed in one hour from now, I'll come and put you there!"

"Oh, you will, will you?" This time she did manage a glare, but it had singularly little effect on his teasing eyes.

"I will—and since I'd probably end up getting in with you, you'd better move!"

"Anything to avoid the proverbial fate worse than death!" she said in dulcet tones. "Talk to you later, Casanova Carlysle!"

Chapter 7

"WELL, I'VE FINISHED my analysis, Jason, and you've got big problems," Vanessa said bluntly as she walked into his office several mornings later.

"You telling me something I don't already know?" he retorted, looking up from the pile of papers on his desk. "I've got hundreds of problems, and you're not the least of them!"

"Hey, back off," she protested, hitching herself onto the corner of his desk. "This sexism of yours has got to stop!"

"There is nothing sexist about admitting that you've put a hex on me and my self-control is wearing very thin." He shook his head at her. "Get off my desk, would you? You're far too close and my fingers are itching."

Vanessa laughed but didn't move. "You're a fine one to talk," she mocked, "after what you put me through the other night."

Jason sighed heavily and pushed his chair back from the desk, linking his hands behind his head. "Okay, Dr. Harrington, tell me about these problems I've got."

"This is an ideal motivation-flow." She handed him a piece of paper. "And this is what you have in Carlysle Electronics." She passed a second sheet across the desk and sat watching him as he examined them with a deep frown.

"Are you sure?" He looked up, an incredulous expression on his face.

"Of course I'm sure," she snapped impatiently. "It's my job, isn't it?"

"Drop that chin, Vanessa," he said pleasantly, raising a purposeful finger. She did so hastily and his lips twitched. "You learn fast, firefly."

Vanessa pulled a wry face. "Can we stick to business, please? What do you want to do about that?" she asked, pointing toward the papers in his hand.

"I thought it was your job to tell me," he remarked mildly.

"Only if you want me to. The problem lies right there"—she gestured at the flow charts—"and it's so entrenched that it's going to be one hell of a job to put right. And that's not all," she continued briskly. "Your administration/union relationships are atrocious—each side is out to score off the other. No wonder this place is such a mess!"

"You are remarkably vehement," Jason said, getting up from the chair and walking thoughtfully across to the window. "Why?"

Vanessa thought for a moment and then shrugged. "I guess because I'm expecting you to be hard to convince."

He laughed slightly. "I rather suspect you could convince a stone that it's made of water, if you put your mind to it. All right, draw me up a proposal."

The intercom on his desk buzzed imperiously and he crossed to it with that long, determined stride, pressing the button. "Yes?"

"A call for Dr. Harrington." Mrs. Macy's voice came clearly into the room.

"You want to take it here?" He raised a questioning eyebrow and at her affirmative nod handed her the receiver.

"Vanessa?" Gideon's insistent tone rang in her ear and she grimaced. "Look, I'm stuck in Cincinnati, probably for the next three weeks. You have to check on that roof."

"For goodness' sake, Gideon, do you never hear anything that anybody says? It's not my fault you're stuck in the Midwest. Grab a flight this weekend and go check on it yourself." She got angrily off the desk and began pacing around the room, still holding the phone.

"I can't get away for the weekend. Look, honey," the voice pleaded, "if that roof's leaking it's going to cause a lot of damage—you know what the weather's like down there at this time of year."

Vanessa was aware of Jason's interested, slightly amused look as he watched the series of emotions that played over her determined face. Gideon was talking loudly enough to be heard clearly in the room.

"Look, Gideon, I'm going to say this just once more. I refuse, absolutely, to drive five hours there and five hours back over a weekend in the middle of March. I am very busy at the moment. I'll go at the end of April or early May—not before!"

Jason turned his back, his shoulders shaking helplessly. For some reason his laughter infuriated Vanessa even more. She felt an absurd urge to throw something at him, and grabbing a cushion from the couch she hurled it across the room. It caught him squarely between the shoulder blades and he spun around in startled amazement. Bending to pick up the cushion, he looked at it thoughtfully before raising his eyes and subjecting Vanessa to a speculative examination.

Her sudden spurt of anger had vanished and she watched him with wary interest, wondering what he was going to do. Gideon's voice continued to fill her ear, but she was no longer listening. Those gray eyes were crinkling and dancing at her, that taut, controlled body poised for something—quite what, she couldn't guess. He walked slowly across the room, deliberately replacing the cushion on the couch.

"Get off the phone, firefly."

Vanessa was grinning broadly now, her pulses performing a ridiculous dance of anticipation. "Gideon, I'll talk to you later," she interrupted his impassioned tirade. "I really have to run now. 'Bye." Without waiting to hear his response, she replaced the phone on the desk and turned back to Jason. He was still standing by the couch, and now, wordlessly, he crooked an imperative finger. He was trying very hard not to laugh, but her own control was not nearly as good, and as she walked toward him amusement bubbled over in her eyes and voice.

"I'm sorry," she mumbled, trying to hold back the threatening hilarity.

"Would you mind telling me just what that was for?" he demanded, putting his hands firmly on her shoulders.

"Well, you were laughing at me, and Gideon was making me so angry—I guess I just took it out on you as the nearest available object. Oh, dear." She gave up the attempt at control and collapsed helplessly under his hands. "I said I was sorry. But it was only a little cushion, after all. I mean, it didn't hurt you!"

"Turn around," the rich voice instructed softly.

"Oh, what *are* you going to do?" she gasped through the laughter.

"Turn around." Firm hands pushed her around to face the door.

For a moment, nothing happened at all and she held her breath, waiting, suspended in the silence. Then she felt his lips on the back of her neck, nipping and nuzzling the soft, exposed skin, sending prickly shivers down her spine, bringing goose bumps to every inch of her flesh. She gave a low groan as the pressure of his mouth bent her neck, and his tongue flicked and darted in the soft indentation under her skull.

"Jason, have a little pity," she pleaded. She wanted to hold him, touch him, feel him, give him back some of this wonderful sensation, but he was holding her too firmly, too far away, and in quite the wrong direction.

"This is what you get for throwing cushions at people," he murmured, his breath whispering deliciously over the already sensitized skin of her neck. After what seemed an eternity of the most exquisite torment, he raised his head and turned her back to face him. He was breathing raggedly, his gray eyes heavy and dark with passion. "Oh, firefly," he said hoarsely, "do you know how good you taste? You're so creamy and soft and your skin smells like the mountains."

Vanessa shivered, knowing that at this moment, if they had been anywhere but in this office with Mrs. Macy outside the door, all her resolutions would have been so much ash on the wind.

Jason released her abruptly and went back to his desk. "So, you're still quarreling with Gideon over that roof? Don't you think you're being just a little unreasonable? If he's away on business and really can't get there..."

"I am *not* being unreasonable!" Vanessa declared vigorously, welcoming the change of atmosphere. "Gideon's just got a bee in his bonnet about that roof. There's probably nothing the matter with it at all. Some neighbors who spent Christmas down there—although why anyone would do that, I can't imagine—said they'd noticed something loose. Gideon's overreacting, and I will *not* dance to his tune. It's over two hundred miles, for pity's sake! If he's that bothered, he can go himself."

"You are an extraordinarily stubborn woman, Vanessa."

"Don't you talk to me like that." She bounced across the room. "It's a typical male attitude—Gideon's work is more important than mine!"

"Stop shouting at me, Vanessa," Jason requested levelly. "There's no need to accuse me of an attitude that I actually don't possess. Anyway, there's more to your reluctance to go to Hatteras than a refusal to dance to Gideon's tune, isn't there?"

Vanessa swallowed, struggled with her anger, and won. "I'm sorry I yelled at you," she said quietly. "I seem to be making a habit of it—I'm not really a harridan, you know?"

"I do know." Jason smiled. "You just happen to be a natural fighter—I'm not, fortunately for us both. Now, why don't you tell me exactly what's bothering you about this trip?"

Vanessa sighed. "It's just that I hate Hatteras at this time of year. It's so bleak and cold and windy and wintery! I'm frightened of going there alone with all that ocean only fifty paces from the door and the wind battering the house—I mean, it's only a few pieces of wood on stilts set into a sand dune on a strip of land a mile wide!"

Jason was watching her intently, but made no attempt to interrupt as she continued, "And as Gideon knows, Noah is a real misogynist. If *I* ask him to do anything, he'll give me a really hard time and I get so furious—and that doesn't do any good!"

Jason laughed outright. "No, I don't suppose it does. Who's Noah?"

"He's the fisherman who does odd jobs around the various houses," she explained. "He's an old, woman-hating curmudgeon, but if Gideon goes to him with a bottle of whiskey he'll do anything."

"I like Hatteras at this time of year," Jason remarked casually.

Vanessa looked at him sharply. "Are you suggesting you come with me?"

"Not at all," he replied coolly. "I was rather leaving that suggestion up to you."

"Oh." She regarded him thoughtfully. "How are your powers of persuasion with surly fishermen?"

"Excellent," he replied promptly. "And I only carry the best whiskey."

"How do you react to a five-hour drive?"

"I love driving. I'm also a great comfort in a high wind." He grinned cheerfully.

Vanessa wandered over to the window and stood chewing her lip, gazing at the busy scene with a concentration that its total lack of interest did not warrant. She could certainly do with Jason's help, and he'd made it very clear in recent weeks that he was her friend. She had begun, she realized with a sudden shock, to trust him as a true friend. The light sexual banter that accompanied the friendship added to its excitement, but was kept so low-key that it no longer seemed threatening. An involuntary shiver prickled her spine, crept across her scalp. It was a frightening thought—frightening because there was something about that tall, controlled man that made it clear his entrance and involvement in her life would not be a casual one.

The decision seemed to make itself. "All right, you're hired." She turned from the window, wondering why she felt so incredibly fluttery, as if an army of moths had found a light in her stomach.

Jason smiled and crossed the room, striding purposefully toward her.

"Jason, I warn you"—she backed away—"if you start anything I'll change my mind."

"Will you?" His eyes teased and sparkled with enjoyment. "I just thought we might seal our agreement."

"Don't tease, Jason," she whispered as he remained still, continuing to look at her but making no attempt to touch her. Although he was holding himself away from her, she could almost feel the heat of his skin under the thin shirt. Tentatively, she moved her hands to his waist. His eyes narrowed slightly, but otherwise he didn't react.

Slowly, she ran her hands upward over his deep chest, sliding her fingers under his tie, between the buttons of his shirt. That hair was soft, she discovered with a tiny sigh, curling her fingertips around it, pinching his bare skin lightly, gently. Still he didn't move, but she could feel his heart beat faster under her probing hands; his breath came quickly, rustling through her hair. She continued her exploration, sliding farther down his body, unbuttoning his shirt deftly until she reached the constraint of his belt.

"That's quite enough for now," he whispered. "I have my limits, too." He drew away, buttoning his shirt again. "We'll leave on Saturday, all right?"

"Fine," Vanessa murmured, feeling suddenly breathless. "What time do you want to leave in the morning?"

"I have a preference for early starts on a long drive, but it's up to you," he said.

"Suits me—five o'clock, then?" She grinned wickedly.

"Five o'clock it is," came the firm, totally unexpected response.

"Jason, I wasn't serious!" she exclaimed.

"I am, firefly. I'll pick you up, then—be ready!"

When the doorbell rang in the still dark hours of the morning, Vanessa opened the door promptly, a cup of coffee in one hand, a piece of buttered toast in the other. She waved Jason in cheerfully. He was certainly dressed both for the unfriendly hour and their destination—tough cords,

Frye boots, a heavy fisherman's sweater over a turtleneck jersey. He looked quite different, as masculine as ever but as if the smooth veneer had somehow been abandoned with the business suit.

"Good morning, Vanessa," he greeted her. "I'll wait until you've washed your face to kiss you—you've got butter on your chin!"

"I have not," she denied indignantly, rubbing the back of her hand across her mouth.

"No, actually you haven't," he agreed with that broad, infectious grin. "You just look as if you should. You don't seem much older than Emily right now, and it's not good for my ego."

"That is ridiculous—you're just fishing for compliments," Vanessa retorted. "Come have some coffee."

They were on the road within the half hour, the trunk of the Mercedes loaded with supplies Vanessa had purchased previously. Jason seemed content to drive in silence, his body easy, relaxed behind the wheel of the powerful car as they ate up the miles on the relatively deserted roads. By eight o'clock, they had passed Newport and were crossing the long bridge over Chesapeake Bay, the gray water rolling in greasy, sullen swells beneath them.

"Time for breakfast, I think," Jason suggested. "Hungry?"

"Not very. I'm still full of toast." She smiled. "But I could use some coffee."

"Keep an eye out for somewhere to stop, then; once we get out of this industrial wasteland and into farm country, I doubt we'll find anything."

It was an odd sensation, Vanessa reflected drowsily. Here she was, driving with a man she hardly knew, intending to spend three days in his company alone in a deserted beach house on a bleak strip of land. Totally unexpectedly, panic overtook her—the same panic she used to feel lying beside Gideon during the long reaches of the night, when they had become strangers to each other but didn't know how or why it had happened, or how to break the mold of their life together. A life that had become a sterile, emotional desert.

"What's the matter? You're wriggling around as if you're sitting on an ant nest." Jason's puzzled voice cut into the suddenly tense silence.

"I think I am," she mumbled.

He gave her a quick, sharp look, and without a word turned the car into the parking lot of a Howard Johnson's, swinging sideways in his seat once he had cut the engine.

"All right, Vanessa, what's eating you?"

"I think this is a mistake," she said baldly. "I want to go back."

"Let's go inside, shall we?" Jason suggested quietly. He strode around to her side of the car, opened the door, and, leaning across her, pressed the release button on her seat belt. An imperative thumb jerked. "Come on, Vanessa. I need breakfast, even if you don't, and I refuse to discuss this in the middle of a parking lot in the freezing cold."

Not having much choice, she scrambled out of the car, allowing him to take her hand in a firm, unyielding grip as he walked briskly toward the red-roofed building. Inside, they followed a smiling hostess to a small table and took their places in silence. The coffee pot appeared almost immediately, and Vanessa took a quick, comforting gulp of the steaming liquid.

"Are you eating?" Jason's voice was calm, polite, as the waitress hovered smiling beside them.

"No, thank you." She shook her head. "Some orange juice, though, please."

The waitress disappeared with their order and Jason leaned back in his chair, appearing totally relaxed as he regarded her quizzically over his coffee cup.

Vanessa dropped her eyes to the paper placemat and began restlessly to trace the pattern with the point of her knife as reality reasserted itself. Jason Carlysle was *not* Gideon Clarke. In a strange sort of way, she felt she knew Jason better than she had ever known Gideon. If she couldn't trust Jason, whom could she trust? She had to lose this irrational fear sometime, to drop the defenses so carefully constructed to protect herself.

A large hand reached across the table, covered hers, gently but very firmly removed the knife. "You look like a naughty little girl who's expecting a well-deserved scolding." Laughter lurked in the deep voice as a long finger lifted her chin. "Come on, now. Tell me all about it. I won't scold, I promise."

At that, she smiled reluctantly. "That's a fairly accurate description of how I feel." His finger remained on her chin, forcing her to look at him. There was no laughter in his intent scrutiny, but there was something remarkably like compassion and the promise of understanding.

"I'm sorry," she went on quietly. "I've just had an utterly foolish and totally unexpected attack of the mean reds."

"Of the whats?" Jason exclaimed, turning quickly to smile his thanks as the waitress placed a laden plate in front of him.

"Oh, it's a panicky, claustrophobic sort of feeling," she explained distractedly, once they were alone again. "Not a bit like the 'blues'—much nastier. But they've gone away now." Chased away by that calm understanding of yours, she thought, as the slow warmth of reassurance spread through her. "Do you think I could have that piece of bacon?"

"Which piece?" Jason looked at his plate, startled by the abrupt change in her tone.

"That crispy little bit, over there by the tomato."

"Impossible woman!" He grinned. "Where will it end? First you try to steal the last oyster that's rightfully mine, and now you want my breakfast. Open up, then."

Vanessa obediently opened her mouth to receive the tasty morsel as he popped it between her teeth. "And a piece of toast, if you can spare it," she mumbled.

Jason buttered a small triangle. "Jelly?"

"No, thanks, that's good." Why on earth was she so hungry all of a sudden?

Jason returned his attention to his plate and they ate in companionable silence. Then, abruptly, Jason put down his knife and fork and looked at her searchingly across the table. "Am I to know, firefly, what caused this attack of the mean reds?"

"If you really want to know, I'll tell you. But I feel kind of embarrassed about it."

"Mmmm. A touch of the 'Gideons,' I presume? You

don't need to answer that—it's written all over your face."
His eyes narrowed as he regarded her shrewdly.

A slight flush crept into her pale cheeks, but she returned
the look steadily.

"One of these days, Vanessa, you're going to have to
bring all those feelings into the open and take a good look
at them. You can't carry the residue of a failed marriage
around forever."

"You sound like Jilly," she observed softly.

"Yes, well, as I've had occasion to remark before, Jilly
is a very sensible woman."

"And I'm not?" Her eyes flashed a challenge.

"Not all the time," he responded calmly. "But then, none
of us are. Life would be very boring if we were." He grinned
and pushed back his chair. "Come on, let's get this show
on the road."

The narrow strip of land arrowing its way between Pam-
lico Sound on one side and the gray Atlantic Ocean on the
other was as bleak and as desolate as Vanessa had known
it would be. Sand dunes, scrub land, pathetic, straggly bushes
trying to scratch an existence out of the thin, sandy terrain
met the eye in all directions. In the summer, somehow, this
became a beautiful, semideserted, peaceful spot for lying
around on the wide expanse of empty beach, sailing and
snorkeling in the Sound, taking long rambles through the
scrub, bird-watching, surfing, fishing, swimming carefully
in the dangerous, current-ridden ocean. But at this time of
year, it was like some almost forgotten outpost of civili-
zation, battered and eroded by the menace of wild, un-
compromising elements.

Jason showed no inclination to make conversation; oc-
casionally Vanessa felt his quick sideways glance, but whenever she turned to look at him his eyes were fixed on the
totally deserted, narrow road ahead. They drove through
the tiny village at the very end of the spit—a village now
shut up and blind, although the small supermarket was still
open. Vanessa directed Jason down the narrow, sandy track
toward the beach, past the few now empty summer houses

standing like storks on their high stilts, bravely facing out to sea.

They stopped at the farthest house, right on the beach. The sound of the ocean hissing and crashing against the shore filled Vanessa's ears as she got out of the car; the wind grabbed her hair and her breath, threw damp sea air and gritty bits of sand against her face, in her mouth. All her anger at Gideon rose again—she did not want to be here, even with Jason.

He gave her a sharp look and frowned at her set face and tight lips, but said only, "Why don't you open up and I'll bring in the stuff from the trunk?"

She climbed the flight of steps to the narrow front deck, unlocked the door, cursing under her breath as the damp wood stuck, giving it a vicious thump with her hip that she immediately regretted—it hurt her more than it did the door and did nothing for her temper.

The damp, musty, unlived-in smell hit her immediately on entering the house. Jason followed, his arms full of cartons that he dumped on the long dining table. The living area was all open-plan—kitchen, dining room, and living room in one. Bedrooms and bathrooms opened off on either side. Muttering, Vanessa fiddled with the central heating control, listening irritably for the sound of the furnace leaping into life.

"It smells awful in here," she complained. "I'm going to open the back door and to hell with it if we lose some heat; the place needs airing." She stomped over to the door opening onto the large back deck overlooking the beach and the ocean.

"Here, let me do that." Jason appeared behind her as she wrestled with the stiff bolts. She moved away and began to wander around.

"Just look at the state of this!" She ran a disdainful finger around the edge of the kitchen sink. "It's full of congealed grease. No one's cleaned up around here since the last tenants. I'll bet the oven's filthy, too!"

Jason continued to bring things in from the car in silence as she proceeded with her tour, her voice rising with indignation at each new horror. "There's an inch of sand in the tub! Those agency people were supposed to clean the place up at the end of the summer. It's going to take me all weekend to make it habitable again, and then Gideon will come charging down and mess it all up again and not even notice!"

Hitching herself up onto her knees on the counter top she began to fill the high cabinets with supplies as Jason brought them in. "And another thing..."

"Don't tell me there's more." Jason sighed wearily, but she was too full of her own irritation to heed him.

"Gideon will come down here with a group of friends or his latest girl friend; they'll eat everything in sight and won't even think of replacing this stuff." She slammed a can of asparagus tips onto the shelf.

"Vanessa, just how long is this going to go on?" Jason interrupted.

"Is what going to go on?" she demanded crossly.

"This diatribe of yours. It's not particularly constructive, is it?"

Vanessa swiveled to face him from her precarious perch. "I guess not," she said slowly. "But it does relieve my feelings."

"It doesn't do much for mine," he said evenly. "You may be angry with Gideon, but I don't see why I should be on the receiving end. Hey, get off there!" He moved swiftly, lifting her with firm hands off the counter top, holding her for a moment in the air as if she weighed no more than a kitten.

"Put me down," she protested.

Jason set her on her feet. "You looked like an infuriated leprechaun sitting up there." He grinned. "That red hair all over the place and those green eyes flashing. Now, put your hands behind you on the counter and keep them there, while I endeavor to cure your irritability."

Vanessa's involuntary laugh was stopped by his mouth coming down hard against hers, keeping it shut with determined pressure. He kissed her until her lips felt bruised and tingling. His hands were on hers, keeping them on the counter at her back, and she couldn't move her head, which was bent backward. Eventually, Jason released her and gave her shoulders a slight shake.

"No more nonsense, firefly—agreed?"

She nodded, running a hand over her swollen lips. "You sure do have some unusual prescriptions for treating ailments of the spirit, Dr. Carlysle," she said with a slightly stiff smile.

"I've written my own medical dictionary," he replied smoothly. "Now, let's deal with this long list of complaints, all right? You get the sand out of the tub and I'll scrub the sink."

"It's actually not as bad as I made out," she confessed guiltily, as he rolled up his sleeves and reached for the scouring powder on the table.

"Then we'll be finished all the sooner," he declared cheerfully, "and can go deal with the recalcitrant fisherman."

"Not till tomorrow. Sunday's the only day Noah doesn't go out in his fishing boat," she explained, moving toward a tall closet. "Which bedroom do you want? There's the master bedroom on the right facing the ocean, and two smaller ones on the left—one at the back, one at the front, facing the lane and the Sound, with a connecting bathroom."

"I'll take the little one at the back," Jason responded easily.

"Have the master bedroom, in that case, it's more comfortable. I'll have the one at the front."

"Nonsense," he said briskly. "The master bedroom's yours—this is your house, after all."

"No, I insist." Vanessa began to sort through sheets in the tall linen closet, thankful that he couldn't see her face or the slight tremor in her hands.

"Now why would you want the little room at the front?" Jason mused, running the faucet in the now sparkling sink.

"It's farther from the ocean," Vanessa explained. "I can't sleep with those monstrous waves bellowing and crashing just under the window. Childish, isn't it?" She gave a short, self-conscious half laugh as she headed, arms full of sheets, toward the master bedroom.

"Not particularly. We all have our terrors. I'm not about to throw the first stone."

Vanessa stopped in the doorway, turned slowly toward him. "You have them, too?"

"Sure." He smiled gently. "I'm petrified of horses—I'll go out of my way to avoid one! I don't like cows, either," he added with a grin.

Vanessa laughed. "That makes me feel a lot better."

"What I can't understand, though," Jason persisted, "is why you have deliberately put yourself in a position where you can't avoid your terrors. Why, in the name of goodness, do you own half of this house? Nothing could be worse for someone who doesn't like the elements."

"Gideon loves it," she said shortly. "His need for it seemed greater at the time than my silly, irrational fears. Besides, I thought if I faced up to them, they'd go away. I was wrong—so I'll sleep at the front."

Jason shrugged. "If that's what you want."

Vanessa hastily censored thoughts of what she really wanted.

Chapter 8

"WIND'S GETTING UP." Vanessa walked, many hours later, over to the back door, gazing into the starless, moonless evening, listening to the moan and whine of the wind around the fragile structure, the relentless roar of the ocean as it spewed itself onto the sand. Absently, she rubbed her upper arms, crossed protectively over her breasts.

"It's Hatteras in March. Only what you'd expect, after all." Jason came to stand behind her, his hands resting on her shoulders, his long fingers exerting firm pressure through the thin silk of her turquoise silk kimono. "I did tell you I was a great comfort in a high wind," he whispered into her hair.

"Yes you did, and you are." She moved away from the window and away from that soft, enticing voice. "I couldn't have come here alone."

"No, I realize that now." Jason stood still where she had left him, looking out into the night. "I can't understand why the devil Gideon insisted."

"It's not really his fault." She shrugged and began to fill the coffeepot. "I never really told him directly how I felt." Not that he asked, either, she added silently. Unlike Jason Carlysle, who seemed to see into her very soul at times.

"Who plays chess?" Jason walked over to the coffee table and picked up a pawn from the checkered board, examining it carefully.

"Gideon and I used to play a lot. We had to give up, though." Vanessa chuckled. "We both hate to lose and we're so evenly matched that the board became a veritable battle-ground."

"Which hand?" Jason held out clenched fists toward her, and with a laugh she indicated the right one. He revealed a white pawn. "You win the draw." He replaced the black and white pawns on the board.

"I hate being white for the first time when I've never played with someone before." Vanessa dropped cross-legged to the floor behind the white pieces as Jason took his place on the sofa across from her. "It's much more comfortable to respond to someone else's initiative—gives me time to decide what sort of opponent I've got."

"Well, Madam Psychologist, you picked fair and square." He grinned. "And white does, technically at least, have the advantage."

Vanessa didn't respond, merely frowned at the board. Should she make a conventional opening? Or try something totally unexpected? A swift, internal smile and she moved pawn to king four—she'd play it safe the first time around. Jason made the book response and they exchanged a quick, conspiratorial smile.

Three hours and three games later, Vanessa surveyed her options in the end game on the now almost deserted board. With a slight shake of her head, she tipped over her king in the traditional gesture of resignation and held out her hand to the still figure opposite.

"Why didn't you go for a draw?" Jason squeezed her hand. "You could have forced one."

"Forcing a draw always seems so ungenerous, and I'd hate you to think I was a sore loser." She laughed, stretched, and yawned deeply. "Two to you and one to me—I'll get my revenge tomorrow."

"Want a nightcap?" Jason strode over to the bar.

"No, thanks, I think I'll just turn in. My muscles ache after all that scrubbing, and I need to fortify myself to deal with Noah tomorrow." Feeling suddenly, unaccountably awkward, she moved quickly toward the bedroom door at the front of the house.

"Hey!" The soft exclamation arrested her and she turned slowly. "Come and say good night properly."

Slowly, she came toward him, a slight, shy smile curving her lips.

Mischief lurked in his eyes as he took her face between his hands. "We'll keep it very chaste tonight—given the temptations of our situation." His lips brushed hers so lightly that the kiss might almost not have happened. "Dream sweetly, Vanessa."

"And you," she responded softly as he continued to hold her face. For a second, his eyes darkened.

"Oh, I will," he whispered huskily. "Just as I have every night since I met you. And one day they'll be more than dreams."

She was abruptly released and he turned back to the bar. Vanessa stood for a second, wanting to say something but unsure exactly what. Then, with a quick shrug, she went resolutely into her bedroom.

She fell asleep quickly, but not for long. The mournful howling of the wind as it increased in force brought her into heart-pounding wakefulness. The very house seemed to shake on its long stilts under the remorseless battering. Images of hurricanes and tidal waves ripping apart the narrow strip of land (as had once happened) filled her overactive imagination. She could almost see the roof being torn off, the house flying through the air as the ocean, finally out of control, broke through the sand dunes to engulf and smother her. She snapped on the bedside light, sat up in the narrow single bed, hugging her drawn-up knees. It was going to be a long night.

Jason opened the door without knocking and stood, hair tousled, face rumpled with sleep, looking at her. "Mmm. Thought as much," he remarked with grim satisfaction. "It is a bit wild out there, isn't it?"

Vanessa nodded, registering the powerful bare chest and shoulders, the fact that his pajama trousers still carried the sharp crease of the iron. Obviously, he didn't sleep in them. That thought reminded her that she was, as usual, naked under the quilt.

"Hurry up, then," Jason said briskly. "Put on a nightdress, or something, and come into the other bedroom."

"But—"

"Listen, I'm not prepared to sit up with you all night and neither am I prepared to leave you alone staring into space, imagining all sorts of catastrophic horrors. There's an old custom, known as 'bundling.' Ever heard of it?"

She shook her head dumbly.

"Sixteenth-century habit, I think." He grinned. "Everyone in the same bed, strangers and all. In the interests of economy, if I remember my social history, but I'm sure it cut down on the nightmares, too." With that, he turned and left the room.

Vanessa got slowly out of bed. She had a nightdress somewhere—a Gothic horror of flannel and lace that her grandmother had sent her for her birthday years ago. She and Gideon had laughed until they'd cried when she'd opened the parcel. Since they always celebrated her August birthday on Hatteras, the nightgown had remained shoved at the back of the linen closet ever since.

A quick glance in the mirror as she tied the ribbons at the neck was not reassuring. Laughter welled in her chest. The voluminous garment had enough fabric to cover three people simultaneously. On Vanessa, it was like a tent, and not an inch of her skin from her neck down was visible.

Jason's face was a study as she walked, with a degree of confidence she didn't feel, into the master bedroom.

"Good Lord! What a revolting garment!" He shook his head in disbelief.

"You're insulting my grandmother," Vanessa declared with dignity, trying to control her own shaking shoulders.

"That's your grandmother's nightdress?"

"No," she denied indignantly, then qualified, "at least, I don't think it is. It was a birthday present."

"Talk about armor-plating!" Jason turned back to the bed, swiftly placing a pillow down the middle, underneath the blankets. "Which side do you want?"

Vanessa surveyed the bed. It was a full seven feet wide—one of the first things she and Gideon had bought. "I usually sleep on the left."

"That's fortunate—since I prefer the right." Jason pulled back the covers and swung himself neatly onto the bed. "Are you going to stand there all night?"

"No . . . only . . . Jason, this is ridiculous!" She climbed into her side, pulling the covers up in a comforting band around her neck.

"Got a better suggestion?" He rolled over and flicked the light switch, plunging the room into darkness.

"No," she muttered, wondering why she felt as if she were back at summer camp. Laughter gurgled in her voice. "This is very cozy. Shall we tell ghost stories?"

"One more word out of you, Vanessa Harrington, and you'll find yourself in that ridiculous nightgown spending the rest of the night on the beach! There are only two things I like to do in bed, and since one of those is not an option right now, I'd like to do the other; so go to sleep!"

"'Night." Vanessa lay in the dark listening to the wind and the crash of the ocean breakers. The sound was as loud as ever, but somehow no longer intrusive. She was safe and warm, all fears chased under the rug by this calm, wise, understanding presence so close to her in the big bed.

Since Gideon, she had held back from all emotional intimacy with anyone except Jilly. Jilly was her true friend, one who would listen, criticize certainly, but always sympathize and struggle for understanding, just as Vanessa did for her. But now Jason, too, had begun to play that role in her life—prompted by what could only be a deep core of liking. A soft glow of pleasure and excitement spread through her—liking was so much harder than loving. One wasn't swept into "like" the way one was supposedly swept into "love." A rush of tenderness overwhelmed her, a need to express these feelings, to share herself with him and to share in his self. Softly, she began to untie the ribbons at her neck and wrists, then gingerly she eased the voluminous folds of material upward. A swift, deft movement and the nightgown was cast to the floor.

"What *are* you doing, Vanessa?" Jason's voice cut through the darkness. "You're such a fidget!"

Vanessa smiled, kept her voice light, matter-of-fact. "I

was just taking off Granny's gown. It's far too prickly to sleep in."

There was a short silence. Then: "Let me make sure I've got this straight. You are now lying in this bed, naked, separated from me by this flimsy pillow. Right?"

"Right," she affirmed.

"Close your eyes for a minute, I'm going to turn on the light."

Vanessa shut her eyes against the sudden brightness, opening them slowly as they became accustomed to the soft glow of the muted bedside lamp.

Jason was leaning over her, his elbows resting on the dividing pillow, his chin propped in the palms of his hands. "Firefly," he said, smiling, "you sure do pick some unusual codes."

"They're not hard to crack, though." She smiled back.

"No." A long finger reached for her forehead, began a slow, circular massage of her temples. "Not scared anymore, my sweet?"

"No." Her own hand fought its way out of the confining sheet to run a slow caress over his lips. "I haven't been for a long time; it's just taken me a while to realize it."

The deft fingers continued to play over her face. "I want to look at you, Vanessa. May I?" His voice seemed, if possible, even deeper, and his eyes smoldered with smoky intensity.

"I can't imagine why else we're here," she riposted lightly, her body beginning to glow as her nipples peaked under the sheet.

"Well, now," he drawled lazily. "And I thought we were here to repair a leaky roof and do a general cleanup!"

His hand reached for the covers at her neck and at a snail's pace drew them down. It hovered less than an inch from her skin but came no closer. Her breasts were revealed little by little; Jason's eyes narrowed but he said nothing. Vanessa lay breathlessly still—this was the most extraordinary sensation; she was being peeled, laid bare to the soft, appraising scrutiny of his eyes. Waves of joy and generosity poured over her—for this moment they belonged to each other; they would give and receive of each other in the ultimate glory of sharing.

The covers now reached her navel. Jason's breath rushed across her skin as his breathing quickened. For a long, tantalizing moment he made no further move, merely pored over her body until she could feel herself flushing as her heart pounded and pulses raced. The covers moved down another inch and for a second neither of them seemed able to breathe. Jason raised his head, looked deep into her eyes, smiled with pleasure and anticipation.

"Such a treasure chest, little love," he whispered.

Involuntarily, her lips curved with joy at the note of wonder in his voice. She was giving what she had and the gift pleased. The sheet reached the top of her thighs and she stirred slightly, her muscles tightening against the overpowering sense of vulnerability washing over her.

"Relax, my sweet," the deep voice caressed her. "We've a long way to go yet." The covers continued their infinitely slow, measured progress down her thighs and calves and over her feet, until at last she lay revealed, an offering for those wondering, desirous eyes.

"Mmmm." His soft, appreciative murmur of satisfaction brought every cell and particle of her skin to life. How could she help but feel perfect, unflawed, under that lingering, wondering scrutiny?

"I want to hold your breasts, firefly," he whispered, "to bury my head in that wonderful deep valley between them. I want to kiss that soft, rounded flesh, to take those gorgeous, wanting nipples in my mouth."

Vanessa moaned softly. He wasn't touching her; he had reverted to his original position with his chin propped on the palms of his hands as his elbows rested on the pillow. His voice continued to make the sweetest of love to her.

"I want to caress that little round belly, nibble those pointy hipbones, run my hands through that soft, curly tangle, move those long, creamy thighs apart, kiss the silky skin inside. And then, firefly, and then..."

Vanessa gasped, moved her enflamed body on the firm mattress. Jason was bringing her to the brink of ecstasy just with his voice. His eyes, full of tenderness and wonder, devoured her, and the longing to give herself completely to this large, quiet man swept all else from her mind.

Jason rose to his feet, his eyes never leaving her face. He allowed her the full pleasure of seeing his body revealed as with deft fingers he removed the pajama trousers. She gazed in wonder and delight at the soft, curling trail of hair running down his concave belly, at his hard expectancy rising between the muscular thighs. Her own body curled in on itself, pulsing with desire. He turned his back, folding the pants with tantalizing deliberation before laying them on the chair. Her eyes ran down that long, rippling back, her fingers ached to hold his taut buttocks, to caress the hair lightly masking the backs of his thighs.

Tossing the pillow that had served as a divider to the floor and stretching himself beside her on the bed, Jason propped himself up on one elbow and smiled thoughtfully. "There are so many ways we can love each other," he murmured. "I don't know where to start."

"Then perhaps I should," she whispered, reaching for him with firm, gentle hands. He sighed with pleasure under the soft strokes of her fingers as she explored him with tender wonder. Boldly, she cupped his promise in her hand, nipped and nuzzled over his body with loving lips, stroked over him with her tongue, sliding her body up and over his so that she was loving him with every inch of her skin.

"Oh, Lord, Vanessa," he groaned softly. "What are you doing to me?"

"Pleasuring us both, my love," she whispered, resting her cheek on his stomach, smiling up the length of his body as one hand ran slowly down his thigh, the other palming his nipples with fingers buried in the soft, curly thatch of hair. How amazingly wonderful it was to give this pleasure, to feel the body beneath her touch stir with delight.

"You're driving me wild, firefly," he murmured. "But I think it's my turn again."

"Whatever you say." She smiled with utter joyous anticipation, sliding her hand inside his thigh, turning her head on his belly, moving herself downward.

With sudden, unexpected energy, Jason caught her under the arms, drawing her up straight on the bed, and slipped a firm arm beneath her, turning her sideways to face him, his hand supporting her in the small of her back. His other hand was now on her throat, stroking and massaging the tender skin before sliding down, tracing the hard line of her collarbone, moving ever so slowly to her breasts. He caressed them as he had done before, circumventing the longing, swollen nipples until she felt she could bear the waiting no longer. His eyes never left her face, gauging her reactions, planning his own movements accordingly.

At last a light fingertip flicked the crowns of her breasts and she shuddered, moaning gently, breathlessly. His lips curved again in a smile of tender satisfaction as he continued his exploration, roaming over her stomach, playing lightly in her navel until she was squirming against the firm hand at her back, unable to think anymore, mindless with sensation. His fingers curled in the soft, downy triangle at the base of her belly and then slid gently between her thighs. Still his eyes held her gaze as his unerring touch played its skillful tune on the apex of her desire. Such wondrous, tender loving, she thought almost wildly as, with a gasp, she clenched the muscles of her thighs and buttocks around his hand and he smiled again.

"Want me to go on, my sweet, or do you want to wait a bit?"

"Wait . . . no . . . I don't know," she groaned.

"In that case, little one, I think I'll go on," he whispered. "Your pleasure-racked face is doing the strangest things to me."

She exploded in a sea of molten gold that convulsed her loins, her belly, her thighs as his fingers worked their magic, carried her to the far reaches of joy. Rolling onto her back, she drew the hard body over hers, spreading herself to receive him, wanting desperately to share the joy as he came inside her still-pulsating body. He moved slowly with controlled rhythm, his breath whispering across her brow, his eyes losing themselves in hers. That same smile was on his lips as he continued to watch her, matching his speed and rhythm to her needs, becoming an intrinsic part of her body, her being.

Wonderful things were happening now as the cells of the honeycomb filled, threatened to overflow. "There's an enormous chasm waiting for us, my love," she whispered, pulling him tightly against her in a convulsive hold of possession.

"Is there, my sweet?" He smiled into her eyes. "Tell me with your body when you're about to fall."

It wasn't necessary to tell him, though; he knew, and as the vortex swirled beneath her his movements quickened, driving deep within her, reaching her core as the tumultuous, magnetic void seized them, sending them spinning into an eternal, star-shot, velvet blackness.

Vanessa continued to hold Jason tight against her, reveling in the heaviness of his relaxed, fulfilled body crushing her breasts, unwilling to lose too soon this sense of completion, of total, loving fusion. Their skins, misted and slippery with the sweat of ecstasy, seemed to blend into each other; he was soft and damp within her now and her hands ran a gentle caress down his back, across the taut hips, over his thighs, reaching for the hard sinew behind his knees.

With a deep sigh, Jason disengaged himself slowly. "Let me go, enchantress!" He reached behind him for her hands.

"You're something of a wizard yourself." She laughed, playfully resisting his attempts to loosen her tight grip on his body.

With a grunt of effort, he broke her grip and rolled onto the bed beside her. "Come cuddle," he demanded, pulling her against him.

Vanessa snuggled close to his hard, warm body, locking herself into the charmed circle of their loving. "You are very special," she whispered against his chest.

A long arm reached downward, ran a lazy caress over her bottom. "That makes two of us, little love. Are you comfortable? I'm going to turn the light out."

"I always sleep on my other side," she murmured as the room returned to darkness.

"Go ahead, then, but stay in touch!"

She laughed softly, flipping onto her right side, pressing her back against the long, lean length of him. A hand, heavy with relaxation, rested possessively on her hip, and she slept in the glorious knowledge that, for this time at least, they belonged to each other.

Chapter 9

"WELL, I DUNNO. Mr. Clarke said nothin' to me 'bout no leakin' roof." Noah blew noxious blue smoke from his pipe in the cramped living room of the tiny fisherman's cottage late the following afternoon.

"I know he didn't," Vanessa explained patiently. "He asked me to come down and ask you if you could possibly take a look at it."

The only response was a grunt and more smoke, and she felt her temper rise, her body stiffen angrily.

Jason, who had been watching the scene with amused interest, moved away from his casual position by the door.

"Maybe we could share a glass, Mr...?" He put the bottle of Chivas Regal squarely on the table.

"Name's Noah," the wrinkled figure rumbled, his eyes examining the label critically. "Maybe we could, Mr. Carlysle."

Vanessa choked back an indignant exclamation. She had introduced Jason on their arrival and Noah had appeared to ignore the introduction completely. Quite clearly, however, he had missed nothing.

"Sit down, why don't you?" With a sun-browned hand, Noah waved Jason toward a chair and rose creakily to his feet. He fumbled in a cabinet, then placed two shot glasses beside the whiskey.

Only two! Vanessa swallowed, fighting for control, as

she watched Jason fill the glasses, his face devoid of expression. To her horrified amazement, he dug into his back pocket, peeling off a bill from the fat roll.

"Why don't you go to the supermarket, Vanessa? We need some supplies."

"We do not," she hissed.

"I'm sure there's something we need," he said in a low voice as he took her hand and folded her fingers around the note with a firm squeeze.

"I'll get even with you for this, Jason," she whispered.

"I'm sure you will." He laughed softly. "I look forward to it." Raising his voice suddenly, he said, "Run along now, little one. This is man's work."

Vanessa gasped as Noah, seating himself heavily before his whiskey, muttered his approval of the sentiment.

Jason flicked her cheek with a light fingertip, his eyes teasing. "When in Rome, firefly . . ."

"Do as the Romans," she completed, dropping a mock curtsy, the action made absurd by her tight-fitting jeans and down vest.

"Go about your business, my sweet, and leave this to me. We had an agreement, remember?" He eased her toward the door. "I'll join you in the supermarket as soon as I'm through."

Vanessa stood glaring outside the firmly closed door. She'd explained the situation to Jason and he had clearly taken her explanation to heart, but he was carrying things too far! She stomped up the narrow lane toward the small square and the supermarket. How dare he give her money and send her off grocery shopping? Half of that leaky roof belonged to her, dammit!

She dumped herself crossly on the stone steps outside the store, hugging her gloved hands under her armpits as the early-evening March wind whistled through the square. It was beginning to get dark and the lights in the hotel opposite began to show themselves in the gathering dusk. The Mercedes gleamed dully, invitingly, but Jason, of course, had the keys. Well, she'd walk home.

Vanessa got to her feet resolutely. It was not much more

than a mile and they had only brought the car because of the raw wind and a general lassitude after their afternoon's play. Jason could look for her in vain in the supermarket.

With renewed energy, she set off down the deserted road toward the Ocracoke ferry, turning off the paved road onto the last sandy track leading to the ocean. She'd gone but a few yards when the sleek car drew up ahead; the passenger door opened, barring her progress.

"Want a ride?" Jason inquired cheerfully, leaning sideways in his seat as he held the door.

"No, thanks," Vanessa responded shortly, "I need the exercise."

"I would have thought you'd had enough for one day! See you back at the ranch, then," he said with a cheery wave. The door slammed shut and she stood watching the car disappear rapidly around the corner. Jason Carlysle might be a sensational lover, but he was also the most infuriating tease!

The lights were on in the living area as she reached the house and she could just see Jason's head as he moved around the kitchen. She continued past the house and down to the beach. Sand crabs scuttled into their perfect round holes at her approach across the firm, damp sand at the edge of the ocean.

The sea, never calm, seemed particularly ferocious this evening, hurling sand-laden waves onto the beach in foaming, roaring succession. The long pier was dark and deserted; even the most intrepid fisherman would think twice about spending time out there tonight. Slowly, Vanessa's irritation faded beside the vast elemental strength of the ocean and the wind. She turned and made her way back to the house.

Jason turned from the sink at her entrance, wielding a large, bloody, very sharp kitchen knife. "Hello, you." He smiled.

"Hello yourself." She crossed over to him and peered with a moue of distaste at the large fish he was gutting. "I thought we were having steak for dinner."

"So we were," he agreed cheerfully, resuming his task,

"but I wasn't about to pass up the offer of a fresh-caught bluefish."

"Noah's payment for the whiskey, I suppose." Standing behind him, she slipped her arms around his waist. "You weren't kidding when you said you only carry the best!" Her hands tugged at his shirt in the waist of his jeans.

"I have to say, firefly, that this place has the most appalling effect on you," he commented coolly. "It seems to destroy your sense of humor completely."

"I'm sorry," she whispered against his back, finally succeeding in pulling the shirt free.

"Apology accepted," he said cheerfully, seemingly paying no attention as she unbuttoned his shirt, pushed it up his back, planted a series of fiery little kisses down his spine. Her hands began to play over his bare chest, teasing his nipples, sliding down to the narrow waist, and continuing downward. She smiled quietly to herself. He was clearly not unaffected by her actions.

Jason turned on the faucet and began to scrub his hands vigorously. He reached for the roll of paper towels, dried his hands briskly, and turned around.

"All right, sexy lady, I've got the message. Into bed with you!" With that, he scooped her up, grinning broadly as he held her easily against his chest.

"I thought we were going to have dinner." Her eyes sparked mischief.

"We were, until you started using those skillful little fingers of yours. Now you'll have to accept the consequences."

"You are such a *nice* man," Vanessa declared suddenly, putting her arms around his neck.

"I'm a what?" He looked astounded and she laughed delightedly.

"You're nice—what's wrong with that?"

"Nothing at all, but it doesn't exactly strike a thrilling chord when I'm about to make mad, passionate love to you."

She rested her head for a moment against his shoulder. "I've been such a bitch since we started this expedition, and you've been so good-humored about it."

"Well, you haven't been bitchy *quite* all the time," he observed, walking toward the bedroom. Holding her over the bed, he suddenly let go, and she fell onto the mattress with an undignified bounce.

Those gray eyes gleamed wickedly at her as he raised her legs and removed her shoes and socks. Bending over her, he unbuttoned and unzipped her jeans. With an obliging smile, she raised her body, and her jeans and then panties joined the socks on the floor.

Seizing her hands, he pulled her into a sitting position. "Arms up!" Laughing, she lifted them as he pulled the jersey over her head. She had never been undressed with quite this no-nonsense efficiency before. Vanessa smiled secretly—this was the other side of Jason Carlysle. Last night there had been the soft tenderness, the gentle wonder, the permission asked and granted. But this was an uninhibited, no-holds-barred loving, which Jason had taken very firmly into his own hands. There was no need to think, to worry, to analyze. That had been done—this was a time for total abandonment, for giving and receiving pleasure without reserve.

He unbuttoned her shirt with the same expert competence and tossed it aside. Then he reached behind her to unhook her bra. Slowly, he moved the strap off her shoulder and placed his hand beneath her breast, globing it as it fell out of the lacy cup.

"You have such impudent breasts," he murmured, fondling the satiny roundness, circling the hard rosy nipple. "They jut forward, just like your chin."

Vanessa gasped in laughing indignation. "I may have impudent breasts, but you have a very impertinent tongue!" She reached for him then, pushing the unbuttoned shirt off his shoulders with determined hands.

"Just how impertinent, you're about to find out," he murmured seductively, standing to allow her to unbuckle his belt and push off his jeans and shorts. He kicked them away carelessly, bending to pull off his socks.

"Now, firefly, turn over," he commanded, sitting on the bed beside her.

Vanessa regarded him for a moment through narrowed eyes. Her body didn't seem to be in her control anymore. She was entirely at the mercy of this determined, loving man whose eyes were softened with promise, mouth curved in anticipation as he smiled down at her. She felt the moist presence of desire between her thighs and quivering sensations of anticipation filled her belly, her loins. Slowly, she lay down, rolling onto her stomach, stretching her arms above her head, yielding herself with a sigh of deep contentment as hard hands pushed her hair away from her neck. Jason began to nibble and kiss his way down her back, sending soft ripples of pleasure across her skin.

"Jason," she whispered, uncertain what she wanted to express.

"I know, little love." His breath rustled across her skin. "I want you so much—I want to make you mine, to possess you totally. Your pleasure is my own."

A hand slipped between her thighs, feeling for the wet secrets of her body, opening her, sliding inside, moving with a sudden, abrupt speed that had her moaning with a startled, exquisite pleasure. But no sooner had the glory crescendoed than he continued his fiery way down her thighs, her calves, over the soles of her feet, without pausing to give her time to draw breath as waves of ecstasy crashed over her. She writhed as his tongue tickled the sensitive skin of her narrow arches, ran slowly over her toes, which he began to suck with a rhythmic ardor. Never had she experienced such sensation; she was lost in the world of her body, not one cell left untouched, unpleasured.

He gently rolled her onto her back, and then the slow progress of lips and tongue began once more, upward from her feet. Vanessa groaned again as his hands moved her thighs apart. Holding them for a moment, he looked into her face with a smile of intense satisfaction and wonder.

She found her voice with a supreme effort. "Oh, my love, do you know what you're doing to me?"

"Yes, my sweet, but I'm not through yet." He lowered his head and her senses reeled under the searing sweetness of his mouth.

"Oh, but you are so delicious, firefly." Jason moved slowly up her body, eyes now hooded, dark with passion as he gazed into hers. "I've been tasting you in my imagination since I first met you."

Vanessa laughed suddenly in sheer delight, putting her hands on his shoulders, pressing him backward on the bed with powerful energy, with the desire to possess as she had been possessed. "I hope the reality came up to expectation, Mr. Carlysle!" Swinging a leg across his supine form, she straddled him easily, her green eyes dancing with arousal and expectation. His hands grasped her hips, lifted her slightly, then impaled her slowly. She inhaled sharply, sheathing him within her.

"Getting serious now, are we?" she murmured with a soft smile, moving in slow, rhythmic circles around him.

"Very," Jason stated firmly, raising his knees to support her as she leaned back. With a sudden movement of his hips, he reached upward, catching her unawares in the dreamy sensation created by her gentle circle. She bit back a cry of surprise, leaning against him, resting her palms on the bed beside her ankles, moving her body around and against the hard shaft buried deep within her.

"Jason, I'm not going to be able to wait." Her soft confession stilled him instantly. He continued to hold her hips but his eyes burned.

"Want to roll over and let me call the tune?"

Vanessa shook her head, running her tongue over suddenly dry lips, arching her body backward against his knees. "I want to give to you, my love," she whispered, losing herself in deep, glowing pools of passion.

"Oh, but you are, my sweet, you are."

Her knees pressed hard against his waist, she brought them both to the shuddering convulsions of the end game, falling, at last, in gasping fulfillment onto his chest.

He held her for a very long time before gently lifting her onto the bed beside him, drawing her into the crook of his arm.

"That was some loving, firefly." His breath rustled through her hair.

"For me, too," she murmured softly against his fragrant skin. Something extraordinary had happened to her this weekend—a weekend that seemed to have lasted for an eternity. It had begun in trepidation, progressed through panic, through the gentle growth of companionship and shared vulnerability, and had exploded finally in a cataclysm of . . . of . . .

Love?

She stiffened suddenly, involuntarily. *Love?*

"Vanessa?"

They had certainly loved; they liked deeply. That was surely not the same as being *in* love! . . .

"You're all tense, my sweet. What's up?" His arm tightened around her curled figure, his fingers felt for her breast in a soothing, undemanding caress. She felt her body respond to his touch, even as her mind, reeling under the emotional assault of her thoughts, silently shrieked, Tell him; *share* with him!

"What's wrong, love?"

"Nothing at all. I think I'm hungry. Why don't we go do something about that bluefish?"

Coward! Coward . . . coward . . .

Chapter 10

VANESSA STOOD ON the sidewalk, lifting her face to the warm spring sunshine, inhaling deeply of the soft smells of late March. It was the first truly springlike day, and the birds were welcoming it joyously. Georgetown carried a sleepy, Sunday-morning air about it as she walked briskly along Thirty-fifth Street. A few street doors stood open in honor of the mild temperature and an atmosphere of pleasurable expectancy prevailed in the unsolicited smiles and cheerful greetings of the other pedestrians she passed.

It would be Emily's birthday next week and Jason had promised to take his daughter out for lunch today to celebrate. Vanessa's inclusion in the invitation had seemed both natural and inevitable. The three of them had developed an easy rapport in the past several weeks, the child accepting Vanessa's presence with a considerable degree of enthusiasm.

The cream-painted front door was unlocked, and picking up the newspaper on the doorstep Vanessa pushed through into the now familiar hallway. She walked quietly up the stairs, Jason's deep voice and Emily's answering chirrup reaching her as she paused on the landing outside the open door to the living room/kitchen.

"One *Washington Post,*" she announced cheerfully. "The door was unlocked, so I just came up. Hi, Emily."

The child looked up from the enormous stack of pancakes in front of her and gave Vanessa a maple-syrup grin. Jason turned from the counter top, spatula in hand, and smiled. He said nothing immediately, but his eyes ran slowly, luxuriously, over her. She knew he was stripping the clothes from her body in his imagination and her skin prickled as she felt herself bared to the sensuous, desiring gaze that she now knew so well.

"Good morning, firefly," he greeted her eventually.

"Why does he call you that?" Emily piped up. "I've been meaning to ask, but I kept forgetting."

Jason grinned. "That, poppet, is between me and Vanessa. Are you going to want any more pancakes?"

The child examined her plate with a considering frown. "I've still got six left," she pronounced finally. "I think that'll do me."

Jason laughed. "It certainly should—you've had at least twelve. How about you, Vanessa? There's enough batter here for another two or three."

Vanessa shook her head with a quick smile. "Can't, I'm afraid. I've only got to look at them and I grow outward with the speed of Jack's beanstalk!"

"Mama says I'll never have to worry about my weight," Emily announced smugly. "I've got thin genes."

Vanessa choked. "Lucky you!"

"If you go on eating the way you do, Emily Carlysle, even your thin genes are going to give up the fight," Jason declared with a laugh. "If you want coffee, Vanessa, you're going to have to come get it."

She pulled a wry face. He was standing in front of the coffeepot, a rakish gleam in his eyes. Slowly, she moved around the peninsular counter top toward him, reaching behind his long, lean frame for the pot. Her breast brushed against his chest as he stubbornly refused to move; his hand casually cupped her hip, his fingers began kneading her firm flesh. Desire arrowed through her and her nipples hardened, pressing against the thin silk of her shirt.

"Unfair, Jason," she murmured reproachfully, pulling back. As she reached up for a cup in the cabinet above, his hand slipped up her body and pinched the taut skin of her rib cage.

"Definitely no pancakes for you." He grinned. "There's at least a quarter-inch of spare flesh there!"

"There is not!" she exclaimed indignantly, and then laughed as he turned, putting both hands firmly around her waist, lifting her easily until she was on a level with the cabinet.

"Put me down, Jason—at once!" She kicked her legs, struggling in his hold as he showed no inclination to release her.

"I've finished my pancakes." Emily's insistent voice reminded them both of her presence and Vanessa's feet touched ground again.

"Go get dressed then, poppet." As Jason moved away, Vanessa poured herself a cup of coffee.

"Are we going to eat a real lunch, or just a hamburger?" Emily demanded, carrying her plate into the kitchen.

"Any special reason for asking?" Jason inquired, watching as the small figure in the pretty flowered nightdress carefully put her dish in the dishwasher.

"Yes," the child replied, wiping sticky fingers meticulously on the damp sponge by the sink. "If we're going to a fancy restaurant I'll wear my new dress, but if we're just going to McDonald's I'll wear my old jeans."

"In that case, you must definitely wear your new dress," he said, bowing solemnly in her direction.

Emily danced on her toes. "Can I order anything I like?"

"You can tell me what you'd like and I'll tell you whether I can afford it!" Jason laughed, running an affectionate hand through his daughter's tangled, silvery hair.

Emily made a face. "Oh, you're just stingy!"

The sudden silence in the kitchen shrieked inside Vanessa's head. Jason had gone the color of clay; a muscle twitched in the suddenly drawn cheek. Emily looked like a petrified rabbit but with mulish defiance continued defensively, "Well, that's what Mama says. She says that's why you wouldn't let us go to Hawaii last summer and that's why you won't buy me a horse for my birthday."

Vanessa prayed for a trap door to open at her feet, to swallow her into a peaceful, dark infinity away from this dreadful taut silence in which father and daughter faced each other in the confined space of a kitchen that suddenly seemed far too small.

"Emily, I don't ever again want to hear what your mother has to say about me—is that clear?" His voice was low, even, controlled, and the muscular body was still, apparently relaxed to anyone who didn't know how Jason Carlysle reacted to stress.

The child nodded, her face white under the silvery-blond hair that seemed suddenly to have lost all its shine and bounce.

"Just for the record," Jason continued evenly, "I was not prepared to fund your trip to Hawaii because your mother has quite enough money to do so herself, and I am not buying you a horse because in the last year you have proved quite incapable of caring for a guinea pig! I am not going to find myself in sole charge of a neglected animal, fourteen miles away in Potomac. Now go get dressed."

Emily left instantly.

"That poison-tongued bitch!" Jason hissed once the child had disappeared. His hands were clenched into tight fists, the knuckles white under the pressure. "I pay her *twice* the child support we agreed on! I'll go along with the private school, horseback-riding, ballet, and piano lessons, skiing, skating, summer camp, but so help me, I'll not have my daughter taught that she can gratify her every whim at the merest hint. And I'll not be put in the position of a miserly Scrooge when I say, 'That's enough!' "

"Ease up, love." Vanessa moved toward him, slipped her arms around his waist, and drew him tight against her. "Emily doesn't know what she's saying."

"Not yet!" Jason spat. "But she soon will." For the barest instant, he allowed his body to relax against hers, then drew away. "Sorry, firefly, this isn't your fight. Why don't you go brighten up Emily's day while I deal with the kitchen? Business as usual, okay?" He gave her a slight smile that still carried the anger and tension of the last few moments.

"Sure you're all right?" Vanessa regarded him with a quick, anxious look, knowing that he wasn't but not knowing how to offer convincing support—a few weeks really wasn't long enough to cut through the barriers of someone else's history.

"Fine! Go help Emily; she needs a woman's touch right now." Jason turned abruptly to the sink and Vanessa went swiftly to the fourth floor.

The small figure was struggling with the zipper at the back of a long, flower-print dress. "Let me do that." Vanessa crossed the room rapidly, unsnagging the zipper with deft fingers and pulling it up in one neat, decisive movement. "There you go. Turn around and let me look at you."

The child turned slowly. Her lips were quivering slightly as she whispered, "Daddy's mad."

"Not with you, sweetheart," Vanessa assured her, hugging Emily's frail, bony shoulders. "Cheer up, now. We're going to have a good day—it's your birthday celebration, remember?"

Emily gave her a watery smile and reached for her hairbrush. Vanessa took it out of the small, dimpled hand. "I think you'd look lovely in a French braid," she said, smiling. "Let's see what we can do to turn you into a sophisticated lady."

Under her ministrations and gently joking tone, Emily became once again her usual spritelike self. Not so Jason, who looked strained and preoccupied when they rejoined him in the living room.

"What do you want to do this morning, poppet?" He smiled at them—a smile that barely touched his eyes.

"It doesn't matter," Emily murmured, her restored spirits clearly fading again.

"We can sit around here until lunchtime if you like," Jason said, shrugging, "but it seems an odd way to celebrate a birthday."

"How about the zoo?" Vanessa suggested with determined cheerfulness. "I haven't been there in years and it's a gorgeous day for it." They had to do something—the mere thought of sitting around in this state of tense gloom and despondency filled her with horror. "Or we could go to the Museum of American History, that's always fun; then, of course, there's the Air and Space—"

"Why don't you two decide while I go change," Jason interrupted her catalog quietly. "I need to wear something more elegant than jeans when I escort two such beautiful ladies to lunch!" This time the smile reached his eyes as he tipped Emily's chin, dropped a light kiss on her brow."That's a very pretty dress, poppet."

Emily opted for the zoo, much to Vanessa's relief—it was really too lovely a day to spend in a museum. The three of them roamed around companionably under the soft warmth of the spring sunshine. Jason linked his fingers with Vanessa's as they followed, at a slightly more sedate pace, the sparkling elf leaping and dancing ahead of them.

"She doesn't get too much of this," Jason said suddenly.

"Too much of what?"

"Oh, ordinary childhood things—like spending Sunday morning at the zoo. It's hardly Diane's scene, and when Emily's with me I seem to spend more time scolding her than I do playing with her."

"That's not the impression I've got," Vanessa said quietly. "She likes being with you."

Jason gave a short, mirthless laugh. "Eventually, the freedom of her mother's house is going to prove more enticing than Daddy's well-meant structure and discipline."

"Can't you do anything about it?" she asked.

"I could go for sole custody," Jason said briefly. He continued after a short pause, "It would be a bloody and expensive battle, and I'm not yet convinced it would be in Emily's best interests. A single-parent father, particularly one who spends half his life flying around the country, is not the ideal guardian for an adolescent girl."

Vanessa said nothing; there wasn't anything to say. As usual, he was being totally logical and reasonable, and his pain was very much his own. She was slowly coming to realize that while Jason Carlysle was prepared to take on other people's problems with considerable energy and determination, he was not willing to share his own beyond the merest statement of fact.

"Come along, Emily, time for lunch!" He glanced quickly

at his watch as he called the child, who was hanging on the iron railings of the elephant house watching what was clearly an almost verbal communication between the two enormous, wrinkled, prehistoric creatures.

"They were talking to each other," she stated with a puzzled frown as she rejoined her father and Vanessa. "Not with words—but they were sort of grunting and touching trunks and looking into each other's eyes."

"Elephants are fascinating animals." Jason took the small hand. "They fall in love, mate, stick to each other through thick and thin—"

"They don't get divorced, ever?" the child broke in seriously.

Jason's nostrils flared slightly as he took a quick breath. "I don't know too much about the sociology of elephant life, poppet, but their emotional life is a lot less complicated than ours."

The small French restaurant was packed with chattering Sunday brunch eaters.

"You want lunch or brunch, Emily?" Jason asked cheerfully, opening his menu.

"Oh, lunch!" was the unequivocal response. "I've already had breakfast."

"Oh, so you have, I was forgetting," Jason responded solemnly, winking at Vanessa, who tried unsuccessfully to hide her own grin.

"Mama's taking me to Greenbriar during spring vacation," Emily announced suddenly. "She says we both need a holiday. I think Jakey's coming, too," she added nonchalantly. "He's Mama's new boyfriend. He says he's going to help me with my tennis."

Jason contented himself with a raised eyebrow.

"I could do with a vacation myself," Vanessa said swiftly. "Last summer seems far away! What's your favorite kind of vacation, Jason?"

"I don't take them," he replied shortly.

"No, Mama says that's because you like to think you're indispensable and you—"

"You've just lost a week's allowance, Emily." Jason

didn't raise his eyes from his menu.

"But that's not fair..." Emily began to protest.

"Two weeks!" The deep voice remained calm but carried an implacable ring.

"Oh, Jason, don't you think that's a bit harsh?" Vanessa couldn't stop herself as she saw ready tears springing into the child's eyes.

"No, I don't! This is not your affair, Vanessa."

Vanessa cringed, shrinking back against the padded leather back of the long bench. Of course, it really wasn't her business, but the coldness of his response was surely unnecessary! She glanced at Emily, who was struggling with tears, her face pale and set. But she seemed to have taken the point and steadfastly refused to open her mouth even when asked quite pleasantly what she wanted to eat.

Jason's lips tightened slightly, but without comment he ordered for her and the three of them sat in a rigid, constrained silence. When their appetizer arrived, Vanessa and Jason watched Emily push her food around the plate without eating it. The same happened with their entrée and Vanessa felt her own grilled sole turn to sawdust under the weight of the grim silence. Her one desire now was to get away, go home to her quiet, peaceful apartment, bury herself in some work. Whatever was going on here was nothing to do with her—she'd just been told that very firmly. Her relationship with Jason clearly gave her no special privileges!

The waiter removed their plates, frowning slightly at Emily's untouched meal.

"I'm assuming you're not interested in dessert," Jason said to his daughter coldly, breaking the tense silence. "How about you, Vanessa?"

She shook her head. "No, thank you. I really have to get home—there's a mountain of work waiting for me." It was not convincing, of course. They all knew she'd been intending to spend the whole day with them. Jason, however, refrained from comment, and called for the check.

The dreadful silence continued in the car, with Emily sitting rigidly in the back seat, staring out the window. As Jason pulled up at Vanessa's Fiat, Vanessa turned and gave the girl's shoulder a quick squeeze, but didn't say good-bye. If, as seemed likely, the child refused to respond, she'd probably bring down even more wrath on her head. Jason acknowledged Vanessa's quiet farewell with a curt nod, and she stood on the sidewalk by her car watching them disappear speedily down the narrow street.

"What are you doing back so early?" Jilly appeared in the hallway at the sound of the front door.

"I have just spent the worst, most uncomfortable morning of my life," Vanessa groaned, leaning against the wall, running distracted hands through her hair.

"Come tell me about it while I pack," Jilly said compassionately, turning back to her room.

"Where are you going?" Vanessa followed her, flinging herself down on the bed.

"New York—but just for a couple of days," Jilly replied. "I've acquired a very exciting new case."

"Oh, good for you!" Vanessa exclaimed with genuine pleasure. "How do you acquire a new case on a Sunday?"

"Bill Douglass was going to take it, but he's come down with a virus, so I'm elected. Now, tell me what's been going on before I die of curiosity!"

Vanessa poured out the story. "I felt so mortified, Jilly," she finished, "as if I'd unforgivably trespassed on very private ground! But he *was* overreacting. Emily wasn't deliberately playing one parent against the other—or even if she was, the punishment was too harsh. But when I said so, he was *so* cold! Suddenly, it was as if I were a stranger." She shuddered. "I'll never be able to eat in that restaurant again, I'll tell you that!"

"So, what happens now?" Ever pragmatic, Jilly asked the $64,000 question and Vanessa bit her lip miserably.

"It's the end of a beautiful romance, I'm afraid," she said reluctantly. "I'm not going to allow myself to get sucked in and spat out again—not after the last time. If it's going to be hands off except in bed, I want no part of any relationship except business with Jason Carlysle."

Her friend was silent for a while, continuing with her

methodical packing. "You were beginning to get involved, weren't you?" she observed finally, shutting her case with a snap.

"Yes," Vanessa agreed bitterly. "Shades of Gideon! But I really had the feeling that there was something solid, grounded, about Jason." She sighed and got off the bed. "There is, of course, but there's no part in it for me; he's just made that quite clear."

"He could have just been very upset about Diane," Jilly said tentatively.

"Sure he was, but he didn't have to slam the door in my face, did he?" Vanessa demanded. "It was just . . . just so brutal! Oh, well, never mind." She shrugged vigorously. "Want me to drive you to the airport?"

"No thanks. Tom should be here any minute."

After the flurry of Jilly's departure, a heavy silence seemed to descend on the apartment. Vanessa wandered around aimlessly for a while before resolutely setting herself down to tackle the problems dogging Carlysle Electronics. She still had a job to do there, and it had nothing to do with any extracurricular relationship she might have had with the company's chairman! Work was, as usual, a panacea, and after a relatively short time she became totally absorbed, so much so that it took several rings before the summons of the telephone registered.

She recognized the rich voice instantly and Jason didn't trouble to identify himself. "I know I don't have the right to ask this, Vanessa, but can you look after Emily for a couple of hours this evening? I'm going to have this business out with Diane, and I don't want Emily around while I do so." He sounded weary, strained. "I couldn't live through another day like today, firefly."

Vanessa's heart did a somersault at the soft-spoken nickname. "Of course I'll watch Emily, Jason. Bring her around when you're ready," she said quietly.

"We're leaving now." The phone went dead and she stood looking at it for a long time before beginning to pace restlessly around the room. Now what? He'd surprised her again, and again she was unsure how to react.

A short while later, she opened the door to a grim-faced Jason and a very pale, slightly soggy Emily. They must have had a hellish afternoon! The thought crossed her mind to be instantly dismissed—it was none of her business, after all.

"I'll be back as soon as I can. Emily has some homework that has to be finished. She knows exactly what will happen if it's not done by the time I return, so you shouldn't have any trouble."

Vanessa felt her resentment rise at his curt tone. "Don't worry, Jason. I can't imagine why there should be a problem," she responded frigidly.

"You and I also have some talking to do." It sounded much more like a threat than a promise and Vanessa closed the door on his retreating back with a near slam before turning to the still, waiting figure behind her.

"Come on then, Emily. You'd better get on with your homework," she declared briskly. "Have you had dinner?"

The child nodded. "I had an omelet—but no dessert," she added dolefully, "because I didn't eat my lunch."

"Well, that seems entirely reasonable," Vanessa stated firmly. "Come show me what you have to do."

The child was really too tired to deal with the seemingly endless pages of math problems and, having made sure that Emily understood the concept and method, Vanessa decided to step in, pushing her conscience onto the back burner in the interests of expediency. She worked through the problems rapidly and had Emily copy the answers. She was in no doubt as to Jason's reaction if he found out, but there was no reason why he should.

"Okay, there you go." She shut the book firmly when Emily had transcribed the last answer.

"That was really cheating." The child frowned.

"I know it was." Vanessa sighed, tucking her hair behind her ears. "But at the rate you were going, you'd have been at it all night. Why did you leave them until this evening, for heaven's sake? You've had all weekend."

"That's what Daddy said," Emily stated flatly, then yawned, her shoulders sagging.

"Oh, I see." Vanessa shrugged. "Well, that was a birthday present—I won't help you like that again. Now, let me find you a nightgown and you can go to bed in Jilly's room."

Emily was asleep almost before Vanessa had left the room. Jason had been gone for over three hours and fatigue was threatening to get the better of her as she mixed a drink and returned to her work. It was nearly midnight when the bell rang.

"You look awful!" she exclaimed involuntarily at the sight of his drawn, pale countenance.

"Thanks a lot." A slight smile touched his lips, his eyes. "Doing battle with Diane is always a bloody business, but I think she came off worst this time. Where's Emily?"

Vanessa gestured toward the half-open bedroom door. "Asleep. She was so exhausted that I put her to bed. Jilly's away, so you could leave her overnight, if you'd like."

Jason walked over to the door and stood looking at the still, sleeping figure for a long time before turning back to Vanessa. "Poor kid," he said softly. "I really gave her a hard time today. You, too, firefly," he added contritely. "I'm sorry."

Vanessa gave him a twisted grin. "That's okay. You were entitled to tell me to keep out of your affairs. I'm fond of Emily, but she's your child and how you handle her is not my business. Would you like a drink?" She walked past him into the living room.

"Vanessa!"

She turned, frowning at the imperative note in his voice.

"How would you feel if I said I could imagine a time when I'd want you to make it your business?"

"I'm not sure I understand you," she said cautiously.

"You understand me perfectly well. You're having a very strange effect on me." He moved toward her, laying firm hands on her shoulders. "I never thought I could contemplate letting another woman into my life after Diane. I didn't want to risk that kind of hurt again. But you're under my skin already, Vanessa, like some damn itch I can't scratch!"

"That's not very complimentary!" Vanessa exclaimed.

Jason released her, running his hands through his hair.

"Damn!" he muttered. "This isn't coming out right." With sudden decision, he spoke again. "Look, Vanessa, you are utterly real from the tip of that recalcitrant red head to the toes of those pretty feet. You're a no-nonsense, straight-forward individual with no pretentious frills, no inhibitions—a bit quick off the mark at times, in more ways than one"—he grinned suddenly—"but you're solid."

If this was a declaration, it was the least romantic she could imagine, Vanessa thought distractedly, but it was strangely comforting.

"Would you stop looking at me like that and *say* something?" he demanded impatiently.

"I'm at a loss for words," she replied frankly. "Just what are you asking?"

"I am asking you, Vanessa, if you could imagine at some point turning this highly satisfactory affair of ours into something more permanent?"

"It's a little soon," she murmured hesitantly, "but, yes, I think I could imagine it." Her heart was beating a wild, joyous tattoo, but she reminded herself that this was all very vague and indefinite.

Jason gave a deep sigh and began to fix himself a drink. "I have to get this business of Diane and Emily sorted out and I don't want you involved in any way, so we're going to have to keep a very low profile for a while."

"But that's ridiculous, Jason." Vanessa frowned. "What possible difference can it make?"

"Diane chooses her weapons carefully and quite ruthlessly," he stated bluntly. "I won't allow her to use you."

"I'm quite capable of looking after myself..."

"That is *not* the point! This is *my* fight. I have enough of a problem keeping the mud off Emily without having to worry about you."

Vanessa took a deep breath, slowly accepting that Jason was utterly adamant and she could either accept the relationship on his terms or forget the whole thing altogether. Maybe she could wear him down as time went on; but what was she getting herself into—an affair with some vague hint of permanence at some unspecified point in the future once a nasty custody battle had been fought and presumably won?

The answer to her silent question was as clear as daylight and as painful as a kick in the stomach, yet she knew she would accept it, at least for the time being. Perhaps, when she'd got to know this unpredictable, determined, exasperatingly overprotective man a little better, she'd have a firmer handle on things.

"Come over here, firefly." Jason put his glass down and held out inviting arms. "I haven't even kissed you today." His lips twisted in a painful smile. "I've been so busy punishing people I haven't had time."

"Talking of punishing . . ." Vanessa began hesitantly, still not moving.

"No, Vanessa, don't plead for Emily! I said two weeks and two weeks it will be. Someone has to be consistent with her. Did she finish her homework?" He picked up his glass again, obviously deciding not to pursue his original request.

"*We* did," Vanessa told him firmly, suddenly determined that she wasn't going to put either herself or Emily in the role of schoolgirl with a guilty secret.

"What does that mean?" Jason regarded her seriously over the rim of his glass.

"It means that I gave her a lot of help. Jason, she was exhausted, and there were pages of the stuff!" When he remained silent, she continued vigorously, "I'm sorry, but you asked me to look after her and I did so, using my own judgment."

"And overriding mine," he said quietly.

"Not exactly! The homework's finished, for heaven's sake! That's all you said, after all."

"That, Vanessa, is a thoroughly spurious argument, as you damn-well know!"

"So what are you going to do about it—stop *my* allowance for two weeks?" she demanded belligerently.

Jason grinned suddenly, the dark tension leaving his face. "Would you come here and be kissed, please? Right away!"

She moved slowly into his welcoming arms, feeling his strength around her as she slipped her own arms around his neck. His head lowered and his mouth crushed hers with fierce intensity. His skin, rough with late-night stubble, rasped like sandpaper across her tender cheeks; then, with sudden gentleness, he thrust his tongue between her lips, softly stroking the inside of her mouth with a sweet, tantalizing touch and taste that had her moaning with pleasure.

Her body tightly pressed to his, she felt a tremor go through him. Then, abruptly, he released her and drew back. "It's late," he explained, "and since I can't stay, I'd better go now."

"Why can't you stay?" She frowned. "Emily's here, you've only got to take her to school in the morning on your way to work."

"It is exactly because Emily is here that *I* am not going to be. She's not capable of keeping it from Diane that she and I both spent the night here, and I wouldn't ask it of her."

"But there's nothing wrong with it." Vanessa shook her head in expressive frustration.

"Of course there isn't," he said patiently, "but I do not want Diane getting her claws into you. She knows something about you, but not how important you are to me. It's going to stay that way for a while—understood?"

"Does she pump Emily?" Vanessa asked thoughtfully.

"Yes." The short affirmative came briskly. "So far, Emily appears to have been remarkably reticent about you— she knows her mother rather well; but I'm not having her pressured."

"No, of course not." Vanessa moved to the door. "We could, of course, wake up very early and pretend you'd just arrived." She grinned impishly at him. Jason stretched a long arm, seized the tumbled hair at the back of her neck, propelled her toward him.

"You are a sorceress," he murmured huskily, holding her head in a tight grip, "but the answer is still no! Now, give me a quick kiss for the road and I'll see you around seven o'clock. I'll bring Emily's school clothes with me and take her straight from here."

The kiss for the road was not quick, but it created more desires than it slaked. Though she dreamed of Jason that night, Vanessa awoke to the realization of how much less satisfying dreams were compared with the reality.

Chapter 11

"So, I HAVE to hire a full-time social worker to run this program?" Jason frowned, looking up after his concentrated reading of her draft program, some days later.

"I'll find the right person for you, but yes, you'll have to hire someone," she replied. "Surely you realized that?"

"I don't know what I realized, quite frankly. This is all so much more elaborate than I'd expected, and this middle-management reorganization is going to be the very devil!"

"You'll please yourself, of course," Vanessa said curtly. "You hired me to find out what was wrong, and present a proposal for putting it right. I've done so. You're not obliged to follow through."

"Vanessa, if you stick that chin out at me just once more, I'm going to find some way of strapping it down!"

"Don't you talk to me like that, Jason Carlysle," she flamed. "What I do with my chin is my business!"

"It becomes mine when it's challenging me to a fight." His eyes crinkled again. "So far, I've resisted the challenge, but I can't promise my restraint will hold out forever."

Vanessa regarded him warily. "Well," she said cautiously, deciding not to pursue the subject, "what do you want to do about the proposal?"

"I need to think——" he began seriously.

"Oh, Jason, I'm so sorry to interrupt you," a bright voice spoke from the suddenly opened door, "but I *have* to finalize the details for Emily's party."

"What's wrong with the telephone, Diane?" Jason spoke evenly as he swiveled his chair toward the door, his body a picture of total control, showing no reaction to the abrupt, unheralded intrusion.

Vanessa stood very still, trying to keep her face impassive to hide her curiosity as she watched them. Diane Carlysle was indeed beautiful. It was easy to see where Emily got her silvery hair, although, with a slightly catty sense of satisfaction, Vanessa reckoned that Diane's now owed something to her hairdresser. Vanessa had been cheerfully satisfied with her own appearance that morning, but suddenly she felt plain, uncoordinated, and distinctly shabby beside this vision of elegance in a soft peach cashmere suit, ruffled oyster-colored silk blouse and long, impossibly matching leather boots with a ridiculous heel. How on earth could she walk in them? Vanessa wondered dismally.

"Oh, Jason, you're such a bear!" the bright voice continued. "I happened to be in the area and thought we might have lunch and get everything squared away."

"I'm sorry, Diane, but I have a lunch appointment," he said levelly, still not moving from his position behind the desk.

Vanessa knew that she should leave immediately and discreetly. Good manners demanded it, and *Jason* was demanding it by his studious refusal to acknowledge her presence. But a streak of obstinacy, ably assisted by a lively curiosity to see what happened next, kept her in the room. At some point, he was going to have to introduce her.

"Oh, what a pity." Diane pouted disconsolately. "Mrs. Macy thought you were free."

"Mrs. Macy doesn't know all my arrangements."

"No, you always were very secretive," Diane announced in a voice that sounded remarkably like Emily's when she was quoting her mother. "Oh, well," she went on quickly as Jason, for the first time, stiffened, "I'll remember to make an appointment next time." She turned suddenly to Vanessa as if she had only just registered her presence. Her words, however, made it clear that this was not the case. "Since Jason clearly has no intention of introducing us, we'll have to do it ourselves." A brilliant smile illuminated the lovely countenance as she stripped off an elegant kid glove and extended an impeccably manicured hand. "I'm Diane Carlysle, as I'm sure you've gathered, and you must be Vanessa Harrington. There can't be more than one person with hair that color in this organization. Emily says it's like a dying fire."

Vanessa took the proffered hand and smiled politely. "That's a very charming way of putting it."

"Well, Emily is utterly captivated by you," Diane went on smoothly. "Perhaps you and I could have lunch one day—there are all sorts of things I'd like to discuss with you."

"Uh . . . yes, I'm sure," Vanessa responded awkwardly, now fully aware of the mess her obstinacy had gotten her into but not knowing quite what else to say—she certainly had no justification for a rude refusal.

"I thought you were expecting a call, Vanessa," Jason said pointedly. The quick look she shot him produced singularly unreassuring results. His face was impassive, but there was something lurking in the gray depths of those now totally humorless eyes that promised an uncomfortable few minutes later.

"Good heavens!" she exclaimed hastily, glancing at her watch. "I really must run. Nice meeting you, Ms. Carlysle." A quick wave, a distracted smile, and she fled from the room hearing Diane's cool voice behind her: "I'll call you about lunch very soon, Dr. Harrington."

Back in her office, Vanessa stood irresolute for a minute, fighting the urge to run and hide. Oh, this was ridiculous! She shook her head in exasperation—all right, so they'd had an agreement and she had deliberately broken it. So what? No real harm was done and she wouldn't have lunch with Diane, need never see her again. She sat down at her desk with an irritated thump. It wasn't as if Jason could actually *do* anything except grumble a bit, and in all honesty he was entitled to that satisfaction. She'd just have to grin and bear it.

She didn't have long to wait. Jason stalked into her office without knocking, closed the door with controlled firmness, and stood, broad shoulders leaning against it, examining her in total silence for an unnervingly long time.

"All right, Jason, get it over with," she said eventually, unable to bear the suspense any longer.

"What are you expecting?" he asked surprisingly.

That, Vanessa reflected, was a very good question. The one thing she'd learned in recent weeks was not to expect anything predictable from Jason Carlysle.

"I should have left," she admitted candidly, deciding to take the bit between her teeth.

"Why didn't you?" he asked quietly.

"Curiosity."

"You know what curiosity does?"

"I've heard it kills cats," she said with forced lightness. This clipped dialogue was worse than anything—if only he'd just yell at her, like any normal person. But then, Jason Carlysle never yelled.

"It also burns fireflies," came the quiet statement.

"I don't feel burned." She tried for a slight smile.

"That's because, by some miracle, I'm hanging on to my self-control." His voice was ominous.

"Oh..." Vanessa fiddled with her pen. Now what? Jason, it seemed, was quite prepared to carry on like this. He made no further attempt to break the renewed silence, which stretched thinner and thinner, like a piece of gum waiting to spring back in a sticky, gooey mess.

"Would you just do or say something, please?" she exclaimed at last. "You have the right to be annoyed, I admit it. I still don't fully understand what you're afraid of, but we did have an agreement that I would steer clear of that part of your life and I broke that agreement. I'm sorry, but just put me out of my misery, will you?"

"Come here, then."

She got up slowly, her heart fluttering absurdly, her palms suddenly clammy. How could this man possibly do this to her? She was more than grown-up, for goodness' sake, and he made her feel like a naughty schoolchild! Squaring her shoulders, she stomped defensively over to him, standing in front of the unmoving figure still leaning against the door.

His response was, of course, totally unexpected. Strong arms came around her waist, drew her tightly against him, a hand caught the back of her neck, slid up over the curve of her scalp holding her against his broad chest in a firm but gentle clasp.

"Keep away from Diane, please, Vanessa, for my sake," he whispered into her hair. "I know it doesn't make much sense to you, but I've never been one to wash my dirty laundry in public and I can't explain any better than I already have. Once I get things straightened out, it won't matter so much—in fact, I might even enjoy watching you take her on—but not right now."

Her head was buried against his rib cage, and the clean starchy smell of his shirt filled her nostrils. She felt all the things she wasn't—small, protected, defenseless—and yet at the same time strong, rooted on rock, as the creamy voice made its gentle plea and confused explanation. Was this what love was like? This curious paradox of weakness requiring strength and strength fortifying the other's weakness? Her knees took on the consistency of Jell-O at the thought. She had imagined she could learn to love Jason Carlysle, but the lesson had come much more quickly than she had anticipated. With a supreme effort, she stiffened those silly, wobbly knees, and pushed her head against the restraining hand until he slackened his grip and she was standing upright again.

"You played my game at my pace, love," she said quietly. "I'll try to play yours in the same way."

"I think," he said matter-of-factly, "that we are going to have to take the rest of the day off. A little love-in-the-afternoon seems in order, right now."

"Your place or mine?" Her pulses began to dance.

"Neither. I've had enough of this domesticity—it's time for a little romance!"

"What does that mean?"

He was smiling down at her, one finger lightly tracing her lips, one hand caressing the soft wool of her sweater over her breast. The heel of his palm glided across the nipple, lifting it under his touch.

"It means, firefly, that in some neutral but very comfortable hotel room, I am going to take off your clothes very, very slowly," he murmured. "I am going to kiss every inch of your lovely body, paying special attention to that part of you that tastes so wonderful, so full of milk and honey."

Vanessa shivered, her body responding as if he were actually fulfilling the promise right here and now.

"I am going to touch you," the creamy voice continued, "until every nerve, every cell, every particle of your skin is alive and singing, and when I'm through, my sweet, you're not going to know whether you're in this week or the next."

"Hush, Jason," she whispered in a soft, unconvincing protest as her hands involuntarily reached out, confirming that his erotic promises had excited him as much as they had her.

"I don't know how I'm going to walk out of here like this." He grinned suddenly. "Why the hell did I start that here?"

"Don't ask me," Vanessa mumbled, struggling with her own body as she moved rapidly away from him. "It was totally unsolicited."

"I'll meet you at my car in fifteen minutes." Jason strode briskly toward the door.

"Hey," she said, startled. "Were you really serious?"

"Never more so. Clear your engagement diary for the rest of the day—and this evening," he added, "and get ready to be loved as you've never been loved before!" His soft laugh hung in the air for minutes after the door closed gently behind him.

He was the most extraordinary man! Vanessa examined her diary, fighting for a return to reality as she tried to work out what appointments she had to cancel. Jason Carlysle was quite capable of carrying them both off to the Ritz-Carlton, or wherever, without even a toothbrush, in the middle of a Tuesday afternoon! And she was more than willing to be carried off.

Chapter 12

"GUESS WHAT'S GOING to hit the fan when Jason gets a look at this?" Vanessa walked into the kitchen the following Saturday noon examining the mail in her hand with a deep frown.

Jilly looked up from her grapefruit, stretched a lazy, dressing-gowned arm to take the glossy white card.

"Oh, Lord!" she murmured, beginning to read aloud the beautifully engraved message: "Emily Carlysle requests the pleasure of your company to celebrate her eleventh birthday at—"

"It gets worse," Vanessa groaned, dumping herself at the table, reaching for her half-empty coffee cup. "Read the back."

Jilly turned it over and read the round, childish script: "Please come, Vanessa. Lots of love, Emily."

"I see what you mean," she said. "Cat among the pigeons, fat in the fire—however you want to put it, it spells trouble!"

Vanessa sipped her coffee; it was cold. She reached behind her for the pot.

"What are you going to do?" Jilly inquired. "I mean, you don't have to show it to him, do you?"

"Yes," Vanessa said flatly. "If it weren't for that personal message from Emily, I could just send a polite refusal to Diane and forget the whole thing, but Emily's bound to ask

me about it, in all innocence. She doesn't know Jason is
determined to keep me away from Diane. She'll spill it out
in the middle of some meal or other and we'll all end up
with violent indigestion!"

"Is Diane really *that* awful?" Jilly asked curiously.

"I guess so." Vanessa shrugged. "I mean, Jason doesn't
strike me as particularly paranoid; does he to you?"

"Nope."

"I've only met her once. She didn't *seem* too bad—a
bit brittle, perhaps, but not some long-taloned descendant
of Lucretia Borgia!" She picked up the card again, holding
it distastefully between long fingers. "Jason's already livid
about the party. Diane arranged it without consulting him until it was a *fait accompli,* got Emily so excited that he couldn't,
in all fairness, put a stop to it. But he feels, quite rightly in
my opinion, that this sort of all-evening cocktail-party affair—at the Sheraton-Carlton, for goodness' sake—is utterly
unsuitable for an eleven-year-old."

Jilly contented herself with a brief assenting nod.

"He suspects," Vanessa continued slowly, "that Diane's
just using Emily's birthday as an excuse to throw her own
party, with him footing the bill."

"Nasty!" Jilly breathed.

"You said it!" Vanessa drained her coffee and put the
cup on the table with a barely controlled thump. "The real
issue, Jilly, is that this would never have happened if I
hadn't insisted on meeting the woman. It gave her an opening, which was exactly what Jason was trying to avoid. I
still don't know quite why, but I feel as guilty as sin."

"Where is Jason now?"

"On his way back from Dallas, I hope," Vanessa replied.
"He was due in this morning, but the plane must have been
delayed."

On cue, the phone rang, and Jilly reached for it.
"Hello . . . Oh, hi, Jason." She grinned at Vanessa. "We
were just talking about you."

Vanessa shook her head at Jilly in exasperation but, still
grinning broadly, Jilly continued her conversation. "Oh, we
were saying *some* nice things, sure . . ." As she listened to

Jason's response Jilly's usually pale complexion became tinged with pink.

"Here." She thrust the phone toward Vanessa. "I can't handle him—he says the most unexpected things."

"Serves you right." Vanessa grinned, lifting the receiver. "Hello."

"Hello, firefly," said the disembodied voice.

"What did you just say to Jilly to make her blush?" She chuckled.

"You'll have to ask her that; but you can rest assured she earned it!"

"Where are you?" Vanessa changed the subject hastily.

"At Kennedy. I'm going to make a dash for La Guardia and try for the next shuttle. I should get to National about four o'clock. Want to meet me, and we'll have dinner?"

"Isn't four o'clock a little early for dinner?" she inquired innocently.

"I had in mind a rather interesting appetizer first." He laughed softly. "Shall I tell you about it?"

"Not if you're in a public phone booth!" Vanessa chortled.

"Perhaps you're right." He sighed. "Too much heavy breathing might alarm my neighbors."

"Well," Vanessa said through her laughter, "just to get you onto another track, I have something to show you that you're not going to like."

"That, Vanessa, sounds very ominous!"

"I'm not looking forward to your reactions, either," she stated frankly.

"Am I going to get angry?"

"'Fraid so."

"With you?"

"By extension, perhaps," she answered cautiously.

"Oh, hell! Okay, we'll deal with it this evening. See you at four."

Vanessa replaced the receiver and said to Jilly, "Well, at least I prepared the ground."

"Committed yourself, you mean," Jilly replied, pushing back her chair. "I would have spent at least two days working out the options to a full-scale confession, but then I'm only a lawyer and I don't have red hair!"

"Oh, get out of here, Jilly, before I throw something at you!" Vanessa exclaimed. "You're always so logical and reasonable. I've dug my hole and I'll just have to step into it. At least I know where it is, though, and won't have to spend the next few days waiting for it to yawn at my unsuspecting feet."

"True enough," Jilly concurred. "You've always believed in 'fess up and get it over with, even in junior high. I remember the time . . ." she began reminiscently and then fled from the kitchen laughing as Vanessa hurled a dishtowel at her.

Jason was standing outside the airport terminal as Vanessa drove up. Her heart did its usual double somersault at the sight of him. The elegant dark-blue blazer and pale-blue turtleneck sweater set off his broad, powerful shoulders, and the color would, she knew, deepen the gray of his eyes. His gaze was now lowered to the magazine he was reading, unaware of the people hurrying around him. She honked her horn and he looked up immediately, a warm, deep smile spreading across his lean, craggy face. Stretching sideways, Vanessa unlocked the passenger door as he moved toward the car.

"Hi, sexy," she murmured as he bent to climb into the confined space.

He tweaked her nose between two fingers, admonishing, "Don't be cheeky," as he maneuvered himself with difficulty into the seat. The Fiat was far too small a car for Jason Carlysle—his knees nearly reached his chin.

Vanessa pulled away from the curb, her mind absent as her body registered Jason's compelling presence.

"What the devil are you doing, Vanessa?" Jason jerked forward against his seat belt as she slammed on the brake with sufficient violence to stall the engine. She hadn't noticed the car coming up unnecessarily fast on the outside.

"Sorry," she muttered shakily, restarting the car. "I wasn't paying attention."

"That is patently obvious. Would you like me to drive?"

"No, of course not. We all woolgather sometimes," she protested defensively.

"Well, I wouldn't mind getting home in one piece," Jason replied coolly, "so perhaps you could avoid doing it again!"

She accepted the deserved reproof in silence and concentrated on getting them out of the messy tangle of "Congressmen's Airport," as National Airport was locally known.

Jason waited until they had attained the relative peace of the George Washington Memorial Parkway heading for the Fourteenth Street Bridge, before inquiring easily, "So, firefly, what have you been up to?"

"Nothing that you don't know about already. But look in my purse—there's a white envelope in the middle pocket."

Jason reached over into the backseat, found her pocketbook, unzipped it, and took out the envelope. He made no comment as he saw the invitation.

"Look on the back," she instructed quietly.

He began to swear then, quietly, fluently, and at great length, continuing in the same vein as they drove over the bridge into the city. She made no attempt to interrupt him, but the force of the anger in that tautly controlled, overlarge body in the too small car was an almost physical force.

She drew up outside the house on Thirty-fifth Street. "Do you want to go on in while I find a parking space?"

"Yes. I'll go smash a few plates until you get back." He opened the door, easing himself onto the sidewalk.

"Jason?" She spoke hesitantly. "Would you rather I didn't come back today?"

"Oh, don't be an idiot!" The door slammed with unusual vigor.

Vanessa controlled her resentment as she drove around the narrow street looking for a vacant spot. If she was going to play dart board for his target practice, she'd try to be reasonable about it; unfortunately, her tolerance on these occasions tended to be fairly limited.

When she returned to the house, the door was unlocked, and she climbed the stairs warily, unsure of what she'd find at the top. She spotted Jason in the kitchen, dropping olives into two martini glasses.

"I'm sorry, Vanessa," he said quietly, bringing the cock-tails into the living room. "That was very childish—am I forgiven?"

Vanessa smiled, taking the glass. "I don't see why not—you've forgiven me the same crime in the past. And it *is* partly my fault."

Jason sipped his martini, deep frown lines creasing the broad brow between his deep-set eyes. "That's water under the bridge. What are you going to do about this?" He tapped the invitation with a stiff forefinger.

"I thought I'd leave that up to you," Vanessa stated. "This is your game and I agreed to play it—somewhat belatedly I admit—according to your rules."

"What do you *want* to do?"

Vanessa thought for a minute then shrugged—might as well be candid about it. "I want to go, of course. I can't see what possible harm it could do, and I'm more than a match for that ex-wife of yours, I assure you." She grinned faintly. "You'll be there, after all, to keep me out of danger!"

"Out of trouble, more like," he grunted. "I just don't fancy spending the evening riding herd on you, Diane, and Emily."

"Jason, that's insulting." She spoke with careful control, keeping her chin well tucked in.

"I'm sorry," he said shortly, "but that's the way I see it. Can't you understand, Vanessa? I feel as if I've been totally manipulated over this whole business. I'd already told Emily that you wouldn't be coming."

"Without consulting me?" she exclaimed.

Jason sighed. "Yes, I'm afraid so. I saw no reason to bother you with any of it."

"Oh, really, Jason! Where are you coming from with this protective umbrella you insist on holding over every-one?" Vanessa drained her glass impatiently.

"Diane can hurt," he said baldly. "Want another of those?" He reached for her glass.

"No, thanks." She shook her head brusquely. "One of your martinis is quite enough. If the gin gets as much as a look at the vermouth I'd be surprised."

"Diane put Emily up to that invitation, Vanessa—mainly,

I suspect, to get at me. I'm protecting myself as much as you—okay?"

"Okay! Now let's drop the subject, shall we? It's beginning to bore me." Vanessa stalked over to the window, gazing sightlessly down at the quiet street. Didn't he trust her to know whose side she was on? What on earth could happen at a large party in the anonymous surroundings of a big hotel? She couldn't go on like this, being shut out of every area of conflict and pain in his life.

"Come write your acceptance, firefly." She spun away from the window to see Jason laying out writing paper on the elegant, early-nineteenth-century desk. "We'll play Diane's game just this once; I don't want to disappoint Emily—or you," he added with a sudden, soft smile.

"It's not a question of disappointment, Jason," she said quietly.

"Oh, yes, it is, Vanessa. Disappointment with me! I don't want that to happen any more than I want you dragged into this mess, but at this point I have to choose the lesser of two evils. So come write this thing and put it in the mailbox, then we can forget it until the party. That bridge we'll cross when we get there."

This was the bridge, Vanessa thought, as she stood for a moment in the doorway of the large, crowded room at the Sheraton-Carlton. There wasn't a face she recognized amid the animated gathering, but that was hardly surprising—she didn't belong here, after all. Scanning the crowd, she spotted a group that didn't look too involved with each other to find the arrival of a stranger an imposition. Walking purposefully across the room toward them, taking a glass of champagne from the tray offered by an attentive waiter, she continued to look around her, getting a fix on the scene. By the time she reached her destination, she knew where Diane Carlysle was, where the overburdened tables were, and had separated a seemingly amorphous mass into delineated groups. She was now a part of the room and felt totally comfortable as she stood for a second on the outskirts of her chosen group. Unconsciously, they absorbed her presence, and she was able to slip into the conversation without anyone even wondering how she'd got there or who she was.

"Vanessa! Vanessa! Hello!" Emily skidded to a halt beside her on the slippery floor, eyes shining, hair falling in loose, light waves down her back. The girl was wearing black velvet knickers, a pair of patent-leather pumps, and a pale-blue silky shirt with a delicate gray print that exactly matched her eyes. Diane Carlysle was clearly as capable of dressing her daughter as she was herself!

"Hi there, sweetheart." Vanessa bent to kiss the soft cheek. "Happy birthday."

"How's the birthday gal?" a hearty voice boomed from within the group and Emily seemed to become someone else. Simpering slightly, she held out her hand with a ridiculously precocious gesture, smiling flirtatiously as she murmured, "Hello, Jakey. I'm so glad you could be here." Her long eyelashes fluttered and Vanessa felt slightly sick. Where was Jason's self-willed, spritelike child bouncing around the zoo, arguing endlessly over games of Monopoly, consuming stacks of pancakes? This was suddenly someone else's child!

"I have a present for you, Emily," she broke in swiftly. Emily instantly became a child again, turning eagerly toward her. "Let's go somewhere quiet," Vanessa said firmly, drawing Jason's daughter away from the group.

"I like that dress," Emily prattled cheerfully, "but Mama says you shouldn't wear boots in the evening."

Vanessa gulped, not sure whether she wanted to laugh or scream. She was beginning to understand how irritating "Mama says" could be. Poor Jason, he lived with this all the time; where was he, anyway?

"Is Daddy here yet?" she asked.

"Sure, he's been here from the beginning," Emily said cheerfully. "I suspect he's prowling—he doesn't like parties. At least, not Mama's," she added thoughtfully.

Prowling was such a splendid description of the way Jason moved, long-necked and open-eyed, around situations that he wasn't too happy about! Vanessa bit back a smile as, having reached a relatively peaceful oasis in the busy hum, she took a tiny packet out of her purse.

Emily tore off the pretty wrapping paper with all the excitement of a normal eleven-year-old, opened the small box, and gasped with pleasure. "It's my birth sign!"

"That's right, Aries the Ram." Vanessa laughed. "Shall I put it on for you?" She fastened the small silver pendant around Emily's slender neck as the child turned readily.

"What are you two up to?" Jason's rich voice seemed to run down her back, lifting the skin into tiny, prickly bumps.

"Look, Daddy!" Emily squealed. "My astrological sign! Vanessa gave it to me for my birthday."

"It's very pretty, poppet." Jason bent to examine the pendant closely. "In fact, he looks a lot like you," he said slyly. "Particularly when you have homework to do and you don't feel like doing it!"

Giggling, Emily swung a clenched fist against his midriff, meeting only muscle. He lifted her into the air, laughing into the small, heart-shaped face above. "You have some guests requiring your attention, Emily. There are six little girls examining the ice cream and waiting for their hostess to give them permission to attack it!" He set her on her feet, delivered a swift pat to the small rear, and sent her on her way.

"Now for you," he said softly, turning toward Vanessa, eyes hooded, lips curved, as he ran a long, slow, stripping look down her body.

"Jason, don't look at me like that," she whispered as the room and the people around them faded into a distanced buzz.

"Why not?" he murmured.

"You know very well why not! I have to greet Diane now. You want to hold the umbrella?"

The sensuous, seductive look disappeared as Jason shook his head. "Go observe the courtesies, firefly. Just watch your back!" He turned without another word, shouldering his way through the room, as Vanessa walked toward the laughing group that contained Diane as its sun.

"Dr. Harrington. I'm so happy you were able to come.

Jason seemed doubtful, but it's wonderful that he was wrong. Emily would have been desolate! Let me introduce you."

Vanessa acknowledged the polite introductions, noted the interested, slightly speculative, slightly hostile looks. These were Diane's friends, not Jason's, and she was being regarded as coming from the wrong side of the tracks. Jason was right, of course; it was an uncomfortable experience. But she was also right—it was manageable.

"I really need to talk to you," Diane said softly but insistently into her ear. "Can we find somewhere private?" Vanessa hadn't expected that. "Watch your back," Jason had said, and presumably he knew what he was talking about.

"Why, of course," she responded lightly, and allowed herself to be drawn away into a deserted corner of the room.

"I'm sorry to bring this up here, Vanessa. You don't mind if we use first names, do you?"

Vanessa shook her head. "Of course not."

"Well, I was *so* upset about that dreadful argument poor little Emily had with Jason in the restaurant. You were there, Emily told me, and you tried to get him to see some sense."

"I wouldn't have described it as an argument," Vanessa said quietly, wondering whose back she was watching now.

"Well, it's always happening. The poor child returns to me an absolute wreck! Jason is so severe—she's either lost her allowance, or not been allowed to watch her favorite programs, or spent the entire weekend on bread and water in her room!"

Vanessa struggled to keep a straight face. The idea that Jason could subject anyone to a bread-and-water diet was utterly ludicrous.

"I really don't think I'm qualified to comment, Diane," she said with forced solemnity. "I spend very little time with them."

"Not according to Emily." Diane spoke with sudden acerbity. "I gather you're there most of the time. I was hoping you could use your . . . influence a little."

"I have no influence, Diane, and if I did I would consider it inappropriate to use it," she said quietly. Was she playing this right? She was trying to resist being involuntarily sucked into a conspiracy, but wasn't sure if she was succeeding or even what the conspiracy was supposed to achieve. Diane seemed more than capable of twisting words and thoughts like pipe cleaners to resemble any shape she chose.

"Well, of course you don't know Jason as well as I do," Diane went on. "He's a very disarming man, initially. I understand how you feel the desire to defend him. But I've known him for over twelve years, my dear. One sees the warts!" A light laugh accompanied the words.

Anger was taking over now, and even if she'd wanted to, Vanessa could have done nothing to stop it. It wasn't based on a desire to protect or defend Jason—he'd been doing that for himself for quite long enough to make him an expert—but on a refusal to be used like a pawn on Diane Carlysle's chessboard. It was time to move her knight, and fork both king and rook!

"I may not know Jason as well as you, Diane, certainly not as long, at least, but I do know that he's an excellent father. When she's with him, Emily behaves like a child— naughty on occasion, spoiled often—but I rather suspect that *that's* not Jason's doing. First and foremost, she's an eleven-year-old who takes great pleasure in her father's company and rebels in a totally normal fashion against the very few, perfectly reasonable rules that have been laid down for her." That, Vanessa thought, was a very pretentious speech—but words were both good weapons and strong fortresses.

A hand descended on her shoulder. To a casual observer, it would appear a light, friendly gesture, but her bones cracked under the warning pressure.

"Jason!" Diane exclaimed in startled surprise. "You do have a habit of creeping up on people!"

"The technique comes in the first manual of self-defense, Diane," he said levelly. "Vanessa, I'd like you to meet some friends of mine, if you can drag yourself away from this fascinating conversation."

But he didn't introduce her to anyone, just propelled her into a foyer inhabited only by a few members of the hotel staff.

"Just what do you think you were doing?" His mouth was a thin line, a hard gleam shone in the gray eyes.

"Jason, would you stop this, please? Right now." Vanessa controlled her own anger, kept her voice low. "I knew exactly what I was doing, and so did Diane. All right, she's a poison-tongued bitch, as you said, but I can deal with her."

"You've made your point by coming here, now would you please go home?"

"No, I will not!" One booted foot stamped in vigorous protest, and her chin jutted heedlessly.

Jason inhaled sharply. "Do you have any idea how much you revealed by that little speech? Why didn't you just keep quiet? Diane's words don't hurt me anymore!" His hands were on her shoulders, his words accompanied by a slight shake.

"Take your hands off me," she warned softly. "If you must know, I wasn't defending you, I was attacking on my own behalf. I don't like being manipulated."

"I told you that would happen!" he said in exasperation, still not releasing her.

"And I told you I could handle it, but I'll handle it in my own way. Damn you, Jason, let go of me!" She tried to pull away, but his grip only tightened. Impasse! Short of making a very noisy, unpleasant scene in this very public place, she had no choice but to keep still.

"That ex-wife of yours does not scare me in the least." She made a supreme effort at self-control. "She's about as subtle as a sawed-off shotgun!"

"Sawed-off shotguns are usually lethal," he said curtly. "I don't think you quite understand. Diane is engaged in a covert tug-of-war with me, and Emily is the rope. She hasn't forgiven me for refusing to play the complacent husband—it doesn't suit her to live on a fixed income and she'll use whatever means she can to get back at me. Emily happens to be my big weak spot—in case you hadn't noticed!"

"There's no need to be sarcastic." Vanessa made another futile attempt to break free of the grip on her shoulders.

"I am not being sarcastic—I am just trying to get through to you. That impassioned defense of yours told Diane exactly what she wanted to know—that our relationship goes a lot further than a casual affair. That adds more weight to her end of the rope."

"But she can't use me unless I let her," Vanessa protested. "And surely you don't think I would?"

"Not willingly, of course. But it's possible to be used without knowing it. Diane's present strategy is to undermine my relationship with Emily, and if she can use you to that end, she will."

"But how could she?" Vanessa was genuinely puzzled, much of her anger now evaporated.

"I don't know exactly. If I did, I wouldn't be so bothered. But I have a great respect for Diane's deviousness."

"Well, why aren't you doing anything about it? If she's such a monster, she's not fit to have custody of the child!"

"Vanessa, I *am* doing something about it. But I have to fight this battle in my own way. I don't want you hurt, and you will be if you become involved. When this business is sorted out, you and I are going to start over with a clean slate. Is that clear?"

"What you're saying is that when and if we become a permanent fixture, as it were, our relationship has to be unsullied by any of the pain and conflict that's been a part of your life for the last ten years or so—right?"

"Right."

"It doesn't work that way, love," she said quietly. "You can't start a new life as if the past had never happened, any more than I can. I *am* involved, just by being a part of your life now, and there's nothing you can do about it."

"I intend to try." The bald statement hung in the air between them, and Vanessa, with a deep, internal sigh, resigned herself. If he wouldn't let her in voluntarily, she could hardly force entrance. She could try to go along with him, or she could back out altogether; it was as simple as that.

"Very well. I think you're wrong, but, as you once said to me, that's something you're going to have to find out for yourself."

"I can't afford to be wrong, my sweet, not where you're

concerned." The deep voice took on a husky, almost plead-ing tone as he tilted her face up to his. Her eyes met a gaze so full of love and pain that all protest left her, to be replaced by an all-consuming desire to love and protect him in what-ever ways he *would* allow.

Chapter 13

AT LEAST, VANESSA kept telling herself during the next few weeks, life at Carlysle Electronics had settled down now. Her presence was at last regarded by all and sundry as a plus. People were now talking openly and willingly to her and her suggestions generally met with enthusiastic, unqualified approval.

However, neither Jason's open admission that hiring her had been the best decision he'd ever made in regard to Carlysle Electronics nor their earth-shattering lovemaking fully compensated Vanessa for the feeling that she was being excluded from an important part of Jason's life. There had been no new incidents since Emily's birthday party, but Vanessa sensed that Jason was preoccupied with something concerning Diane and Emily, and he clearly had no intention of confiding in her about it. No doubt he thought he was protecting her, but she felt hurt and negated.

The whole thing blew up on a glorious mid-April Sunday morning, which had begun blissfully with Jason making love to her while she was only half-awake, and then letting her fall asleep again while he prepared a delectable breakfast of eggs Benedict on English muffins, fresh orange juice, and perked coffee.

After the meal, they sat on the living room floor reading the Sunday *Post* as they waited for Diane to drop Emily off. It wasn't one of Jason's scheduled visits with the child, but by now Vanessa had learned that in addition to the agreed-upon visiting days, Emily paid extra visits whenever Diane found her inconvenient, which was apparently the case today. As it neared ten o'clock, the hour Emily was due to arrive, Jason went to the window to watch for her.

"Oh, God, I don't believe this!" he said suddenly. Vanessa looked up to see his eyes fixed on the street below. "Disappear, firefly!" he ordered.

"What?" She dropped the paper to the floor, staring at the tall, tight figure by the window in utter disbelief.

"Diane has decided to pay a visit herself," he rumbled. "She usually just drops Emily at the door, but today she appears to be coming, too. Do me a favor and hop upstairs until she's gone. She'd like to find you here; I'd like to disappoint her."

"Oh, no, Jason! I'll go along with a lot, but I won't scuttle upstairs like some spider escaping the broom!"

"Vanessa, please!" Jason turned from the window, his voice urgent. "You've got no clothes on, for heaven's sake!"

"I do, too," she retorted furiously.

"You're wearing my dressing gown, and it's plain as day that you've just got out of my bed."

"So what? We're hardly committing adultery. It's one thing to ask me not to make any speeches; quite another to hide me away from her altogether."

"What happened to our low-profile agreement?" Jason demanded. "I'm just asking you to go upstairs for five or ten minutes; that's all. It's no big deal."

No big deal—sure. Vanessa got to her feet, gathering up the newspaper as she did so—might as well have something to read in exile!

Upstairs, she dressed slowly, her fingers numb and uncoordinated. She loved Jason Carlysle with a deep, bone-shaking, gut-wrenching intensity, and he wasn't even prepared to declare her presence in his life as a given factor to the woman he'd divorced five years ago! She'd been a fool to accept his explanations at the party—maybe they made some twisted sense to him, but how could she contemplate spending the rest of her life with someone who insisted on always keeping her in one sterile compartment of his life? She'd been through that once already—in the last years of their marriage, the only part of Gideon's life that she'd shared had been behind the bedroom door. Never again! She completed her dressing and sat in the bedroom chair until the coast was clear enough for her to leave.

She heard Jason's deep voice on the staircase, Diane's brittle reply, the firm, decisive half slam of the front door, his quick footsteps up the two flights until he reached her.

"I'm sorry, firefly. I wouldn't have had that happen for anything." He stood leaning against the door, expression anxious, eyes concerned.

"It won't happen to me again," she affirmed quietly, getting to her feet. "Say good-bye to Emily for me, will you?"

"Vanessa, don't leave like this, please." He put a hand on her arm, but she shook it off with a quick, dismissive gesture.

"I don't spend my time skulking in back bedrooms until I'm wanted, Jason—I have too much self-respect for that. My behavior may have led you to believe otherwise—I've abdicated far too much responsibility and control, but it's going to stop now." She moved with an almost desperate speed to the door, knowing that if he got his hands on her she would end up staying because he would somehow convince her that what she knew had just happened actually hadn't . . . and she would believe him because she wanted to!

Jason moved toward her, but she was too quick for him. She ran down the stairs, heedless of his voice behind her, of Emily's puzzled call as she passed the open door to the living room. The front door was fortunately unlocked, and Vanessa wrenched it open, not bothering to check if it was properly shut behind her as she ran along the sidewalk. She prayed that Jason wouldn't come after her, knowing that if he did she couldn't outrun him and he'd catch her easily at the car, anyway. But she heard nothing behind her and clambered breathlessly into the Fiat, tears stinging her eyes as she pulled away from the curb and headed for the desolate safety of home.

Jilly heard her out in her usual quiet, empathetic silence. "You do seem to find them, Van," she commented finally with a small, sad shake of her head. "What sort of game is he playing, for heaven's sake?"

"I don't know." Vanessa blew her nose vigorously. "But I do know he's not playing it with me any longer. I don't know the rules—they keep changing and I don't know from one moment to the next whether I'm the ball or one of the players! Thank God I'm almost through at Carlysle Electronics. There's less than a week's work left, and I can probably finish up when he's off on one of his trips."

"He's certainly something of a here-today-and-gone-tomorrow lover," Jilly remarked.

"I don't mind that," Vanessa said quietly. "He's got a far-flung empire to run—his absences aren't the problem." She got to her feet with sudden energy. "I'm going to soak in a long, hot tub, read an undemanding novel, and soothe my inner self with a glass of wine."

The plan worked to a certain extent, but not enough to prevent her startled jump and suddenly moistened palms when the phone shrilled at around seven o'clock that evening. Jilly glanced at her, then picked it up.

"Hello. Yes, she's here. Hold on." She held the receiver toward Vanessa, one hand covering the mouthpiece. Vanessa shook her head vigorously and Jilly sighed.

"Look, Van, you have to talk to him," she said in a low voice. "You can't just behave as if he doesn't exist and I'm not going to play monkey-in-the-middle!"

Vanessa bit her lip and took the phone. "Hello."

"Vanessa, would you come over here, please?" No preamble, not even a half apology, nothing but that slightly exasperated request. In fact, it was more of an order than a request. Renewed anger came to her aid.

"Is the coast clear, then?" she asked sardonically. "Shall I use the back door to be sure the neighbors don't see me? I'm sure Diane has her spies out."

His sharp intake of breath hissed in her ear. "I'll be there in fifteen minutes." The line went dead.

Jilly was looking at her, astounded.

"He's coming here," Vanessa said flatly.

"Well, I'm not surprised!" her friend exclaimed. "No man worth his salt would let that sort of provocation go unanswered."

"Oh, Lord," Vanessa muttered. "I suppose it was a bit much. I just lost my cool."

"You sure did!" Jilly agreed emphatically. "Well, I was going to wash my hair, but I think I'll go do it at Tom's."

"Don't you dare desert me, Jilly," Vanessa wailed.

"Listen, friend, I'm not staying around here to get spattered with your blood and Jason's when you two get started! I'll stay until he arrives," she added with a slight grin, "mainly to make sure you let him in."

In fact it was Jilly who answered the door as Vanessa stood in the living room by the window, listening to Jason's calm greeting, her friend's cheery response. Vanessa cursed silently as Jilly declared brightly, "Don't worry, I'm just leaving. Van's in the living room." She followed behind Jason, winked mischievously at Vanessa over his shoulder. "I think I'll take my toothbrush; you two look as if you're in for a long session!" Then she whisked herself away, and a tense, expectant silence fell.

Jason sat down on the couch, regarding Vanessa with quiet eyes. "Come here and let me hold you," he said softly. "You can exact any penalty you wish, call me every name under the sun, I know I've earned it, but come close to me while you do it."

Vanessa shook her head; her throat felt clogged with words, emotions, that she couldn't express.

Jason moved then, rising to stride toward her, lifting her easily into his arms.

"Put me down!" She struggled fiercely in the invincible grip as he carried her back to the couch, sitting down, cradling her against his chest as she kicked and fought, her head buried against his sweater, her body held sideways to his by hard-muscled arms.

Eventually, she gave up the struggle she wasn't going to win. A more futile exercise than entering a physical battle with six feet two inches of Jason Carlysle would be hard to find! As she became still, his hold relaxed; not enough to give her sufficient leeway to escape, however.

"Now, firefly," he said firmly, "tell me what a bastard I am—a thoroughly stupid, insensitive bastard! You can't say anything to me that I haven't already said to myself a hundred times over today."

The soft, apologetic voice was seducing her again; the quiet, logical acceptance of her right to be furious, to be punitive, was turning her bullets to blanks.

Gentle, almost hesitant fingers now slid inside the opening of the silk kimono she had put on after her bath, and with a curious numbness she waited to see what would happen. Her body responded, as always, to his expert caresses, the tender endearments he murmured as he slowly pushed the thin fabric aside, gazing at her still figure with the look of desiring wonder that had never failed to make her feel as if her body was a sacred shrine.

But there was a strange deadness inside her this time. Jason seemed to feel it, and with strong hands shifted her on his knee into a half-sitting position, holding her head in the crook of his arm, his other hand tracing the planes of her face. Nothing was said for a long time, not until he felt some of the tension leave her under the undemanding strokes of his fingers as he massaged her temples, her eyelids, the high cheekbones.

"I'm going to take you to bed, my sweet," he whispered then. "I'm going to show you with my body how I feel. It's the only way I know how to mend you again." She said nothing as he lifted her with him, the robe falling open, away from her, as he carried her through to her bedroom, depositing her with infinite tenderness onto the wide bed, sliding the kimono off her shoulders. She watched as he undressed swiftly before dropping down beside her.

"Keep still now, little love, and let me make it better." He turned her onto her side, facing away from him, and began to play one of their favorite games. Jason called it tip-touching, and as his fingers brushed across her back with feather lightness Vanessa shivered, her skin rippling in anticipation of the next touch, not knowing where it would land or when. It was an exquisite sensation and her hurt feelings were pushed to the back burner, to be worried about later. Then something inside her head screamed in rebellion. Not again! This morning *had* happened, just as all the other incidents *had* happened, although she had allowed herself to be soothed and reassured after each one.

The words came out of her mouth without volition. "We have to stop this, Jason, right now."

"Why, firefly?" His breath rustled against her neck. "I thought you were enjoying it—your skin was dancing."

"I don't mean just this. I mean everything—you, me, all of it!" Her statement hung in the air, seemed to fill the room. She found herself drawing her knees up to her chest, curling in on herself as she wondered why she'd picked this moment for her declaration. Ending a love affair in bed was hardly appropriate! But then, perhaps for her it was. The bitter thought matched the cold emptiness inside her.

"Turn around, Vanessa." Jason broke the seemingly endless silence, his voice quiet and level as usual.

She shook her head dumbly, wanting only to stay like this until he'd left, curved around her desolation in the crimson-shot blackness of her tightly closed eyes.

"If you have something to say to me, you'll damn-well say it to my face!" The voice was no longer even, controlled; harsh anger rasped as he seized her shoulders, rolling her onto her back. "Open your eyes!"

She obeyed but kept her gaze fixed on a tiny indentation in the ceiling.

"Now, just run that by me again, please—very slowly."

"It's not working out," she said in a flat monotone. "It's all very well to say you're sorry for what happened this morning, but it will probably happen again. Oh, it's all right for me to be around Emily so long as we just play Monopoly or go to the zoo! But anything more serious is taboo. I won't be hidden away in bedrooms when my presence is inconvenient and then made love to as if that made everything just hunky-dory again! I'm not getting myself into another sterile, mattress-centered relationship. And don't tell me your recent compliments about my work show that you appreciate my intelligence. The only thing you really appreciate about me is my body, and we both know it! Now, I'm going to shut myself in the bathroom for a long time. Please be gone before I come out."

She rolled over, swinging her legs to the floor preparatory to getting to her feet. She got no farther and wondered miserably why she'd ever thought she would. His hands seized her waist, the fingers suddenly hard as they squeezed her tightly, holding her down as she now sat on the edge of the bed.

For a long, long time there was silence. Vanessa made no attempt to evade the hands at her waist, but remained staring, unseeing, at her knees. Suddenly, she was released.

"I'm too angry to deal with this right now," Jason's soft, controlled voice spoke into the dreadful quiet. The mattress shifted, relieved of his weight, and she continued to sit on the side of the bed as Jason dressed swiftly and left without casting her a second glance. The careful click of the front door resounded in the dead weight of the silence.

Numbly, she pulled back the covers, crawled shivering between the sheets. What possible right had *he* to be angry? She was definitely the injured party at this point. It was a singularly uncomforting thought, and desolation washed through her as she fought her wakeful body for the blissful amnesia of sleep. Eventually, however, she settled for lying wide-eyed in the dark bedroom wondering why she was as she was; why she couldn't find some simple, uncomplicated solution to the human need for physical and emotional completion with another. Jilly seemed to have succeeded. Tom was a thoroughly nice person—responsible, relatively uncomplicated, clear-sighted. He was bright, full of humor, had no extraordinary entanglements in his life! Oh, why did she *always* fall for impossible men?

The shrill peal of the doorbell brought her upright, fumbling for the bedside light switch, reaching for her robe as her feet swung to the floor. Jilly must have changed her mind about staying at Tom's—it was unlike her to forget her door key, though.

But it was Jason who stepped briskly into the hallway as she swung open the door. His face was expressionless, but the pupils of his eyes had shrunk to tiny pinpricks like dagger tips. Vanessa shivered involuntarily as the too soft voice declared evenly, "I think it's time to deal once and for all with this 'I'm only a sex object' obsession of yours."

"I don't know what you're talking about," Vanessa said with forced casualness, and started to walk away from him into the living room.

"You soon will," the voice stated bluntly as a hard hand gripped her upper arm.

"What do you think you're doing?" She pulled away from him frantically, half running into the living room.

"Be still, Vanessa." The smooth, even voice took on a jagged edge as he followed her. "I'm not going to hurt you. I'm just going to demonstrate something to you."

"What gives you the right to demonstrate anything?" she flamed, holding on to the back of a chair as if it could in some small way provide protection against that too large figure stalking her lazily across the room.

"A vested interest," he replied grimly. "Would you come into the bedroom, please."

She stared at him, thunderstruck. After everything that had happened today, this evening, he was coolly asking her—no, *telling* her—to come to bed.

"I will *not!* This is my apartment and you are no longer welcome. I suggest you leave before I call Security." It sounded ridiculous, even to her enraged ears, and Jason brushed her protest aside as if it were no more than the indignant squawk of a very small child.

"You leave me no choice, Vanessa." He advanced on her with a determination that had her heart thundering in her breast as she stepped hastily backward. She could do nothing to prevent him, however, as with a swift movement he bent, caught her behind the knees, and tossed her easily over one broad shoulder.

"How dare you!" she yelled in total, mortified outrage, pounding her fists against his back as he strode with her out of the room.

"Stop it, Vanessa. Otherwise I will be forced to retaliate, and your position, in case you hadn't noticed, is a mite vulnerable right now."

Did she detect a hint of laughter in that level voice? Vanessa ceased her struggles abruptly—they only added to the indignity of her position and she needed to think clearly about this extraordinary turn of events. She would never, in her wildest fantasies, have cast Jason Carlysle in the role of caveman, but it was a part he seemed more than capable of playing—in fact, she thought uneasily, he actually seemed to be enjoying it!

She was dumped unceremoniously into the middle of her bed.

"Now, my sweet-tempered, sugar-tongued firefly, oblige me by staying exactly where you are."

He *was* laughing, but there was a steely determination beneath the amusement that kept her in obedience on the bed, watching with wary incredulity as he swiftly undressed. He bent over her, unfastening her robe, flipping her onto her front as he stripped it off, tossing it carelessly to the floor. She rolled rapidly onto her back again, eyes widening as he knelt on the bed beside her.

"All right, my sweet, we are going to retrace our steps," he announced firmly. "I am going to make love to you as I intended to do before, and in the process you are going to take a good look at this ridiculous preoccupation you have about being sexually manipulated. I thought we'd dealt with it at Hatteras, but it seems I was wrong. Once we get that out of the way, we'll deal with the rest of this mess."

Rage, deeper than any she had ever known, engulfed Vanessa at this calm statement, which seemed to negate every one of her perfectly legitimate complaints. She bounced upright, hurling herself at the controlled figure with updrawn hand. Her flat palm made swinging contact with his cheek as a stream of invective poured from her lips. Jason flinched, eyes narrowing as she struck him, but apart from that he remained still, receiving the battering in impassive silence. When she had said everything she had to say and had fallen into a stunned silence, he reached for her, drawing her onto his lap.

"I've been trying to get that out of you all evening," he said calmly. "I deserved the whole, firefly, and I apologize unreservedly."

"Why did you send me away like that?" she murmured, suddenly exhausted, drained of all anger, wanting now only an explanation that could make some sense.

"Panic," he admitted candidly. "You were too vulnerable, sitting there with those gorgeous, love-filled eyes, lost in that enormous robe. Diane only comes in with Emily when she wants something that she knows I'll refuse, in the hope that I won't argue with her in front of the child. I should have suggested you go put some clothes on and then come down if you wanted to, but I couldn't face a confrontation with both Emily and you—looking as you did. A few well-placed barbs in your direction and I'd have lost my temper. It wasn't that I wanted to deny you, my love, you must understand that. You're a part of my life, an absolutely necessary part of my *whole* life—past, present, and future—and I don't give a damn who knows it; not even Diane, now. But because you are, I'll protect you from attack with everything in my power. If I hadn't panicked this morning, I'd have been able to explain all that."

Vanessa shifted on his lap, one hand tracing the scarlet marks of her fingers on his cheek. She knew all about panic. "I hurt you," she whispered.

"I allowed you to."

For the first time, she realized the truth in that statement. In her impassioned fury, she hadn't paused to wonder why he hadn't stopped her as he could easily have done.

"Why did you?" She frowned.

"I told you, I earned it." He smiled ruefully. "Also, I wanted your anger—that I can deal with. That flat deadness of yours earlier, quiet frankly, Vanessa, scared the living daylights out of me. I didn't know what to do with it."

"Oh," she said thoughtfully, her fingers still running softly over his cheek as if she could somehow erase the hurt.

"However, my sweet"—Jason leaned back against the pillows, still holding her firmly—"don't make the mistake of assuming any precedents. I don't enjoy being used as a punching bag!"

"I didn't enjoy it, either," she informed him.

"I don't imagine you did." He laughed suddenly. "I have just one question. Don't you think that two thousand dollars a week is a rather exorbitant price to pay to humor one's mistress in order to keep her in bed?"

"Oh, unfair, Jason!" she protested. "I didn't really mean it like that. It's just that sometimes I've felt like an appendage, whose usefulness has to be weighed against nuisance value!"

"Vanessa!" he exclaimed, rolling over on the bed, still holding her clamped tightly against him, laughing bright-eyed into her face. "I think that brings me to my demonstration."

His mouth came down on hers, kissing her with a sound thoroughness that left her breathless. His hands ran slowly over her body, sliding beneath her, cupping her buttocks, lifting them to meet him as he slipped easily inside her.

"Now, my little sex object," he murmured, as he began to move slowly, strokingly within her, "tell me what we are doing."

"Loving," she whispered, knowing there was no other way to describe what he was doing to her or the soft expression in those clear gray eyes, raking her face for the signs that he was truly pleasuring her.

"Now, firefly, watch this." The voice became almost curt, his face expressionless as he began to drive deep within her, evincing only a careless disregard for the body beneath his. Vanessa gasped at the sudden change both in Jason and herself. Suddenly, she was a mere lump of clay to be manipulated and used for the satisfaction of that hard, strong body above.

"Jason, come back, please," she pleaded softly.

With equal suddenness, he returned to his body; a hand ran gently over her face as his movements slowed again. "Now, my little sex object, tell me what that was," he commanded softly.

"You, having sex," she replied quietly.

"Did you enjoy it?"

"No."

"Could you have, if I'd gone on?"

She moved her head on the pillow in a firm negative, hot tears rolling down her face.

"Do you think *I* could have enjoyed it?"

"No." She shook her head again.

"And what were you and Gideon doing, when you enjoyed each other?"

She began to feel as if this inexorable catechism would continue forever. "Loving." She sighed, licking the stinging saltiness of her tears off her lips.

"It goes a little beyond technique, doesn't it, my sweet?"

The deliberately brutal phraseology made her wince as she nodded miserably.

"You and Gideon may not have been able to live together, but there must have been something there that enabled you to love each other like this, right? Answer me, Vanessa!" he insisted, when she remained silent.

"Yes, there was," she admitted in a low voice, suddenly accepting that it was more than sexual attraction that had drawn her into marriage with Gideon.

"There. Ghosts laid to rest now, Vanessa?" he questioned softly.

She gave him a watery smile, then gasped suddenly as he drew back, pausing for the briefest instant on the very edge of her body before sheathing himself with incredible slowness within her. His face seemed to melt with love and the exquisite pleasure he was taking, and her own disintegrated as the sweetness filled her. He was holding her against him, squeezing the firm flesh of her hips as again he withdrew to the brink, then slowly became a part of her once more.

Jason seemed able to go on forever, holding them both on the edge of the precipice. Her entire self seemed to shine from her eyes, reaching for that loving self that glowed back at her. She was losing herself in that love, and her soft moans became the urgent cries of desperate need for absolution, for possession, for completeness. She was making incoherent sounds in the back of her throat, grasping his buttocks, pulling them against the cleft of her body as his movements quickened, arching herself to meet him, curling her legs around his body, forcing him to stay still, deep inside her, as the powerful pounding of his manhood pulsated and exploded in a cataclysmic finale that tore the primitive cries of man/woman from them both.

Chapter 14

"YOU HAVE, I SUPPOSE, heard the expression "burning the candle at both ends"? Jilly remarked casually late one night as Vanessa, with a sigh of exhaustion, kicked off her shoes and collapsed on the sofa.

"Are you trying to tell me something?" she groaned.

"I'll tell you this, friend, the way you're abusing your body these days isn't going to do it any good in the long term. You're thirty, not twenty, you know?"

Vanessa pulled a wry face. "I wish you weren't always so blunt, Jilly."

"If you think I'm blunt, what do you think Jason's going to say when he gets back? You've lost pounds, and those shadows under your eyes! . . ."

"So I'm not Superwoman. I've had a lot to do recently, and it's hardly Jason's business if I lose a bit of weight!"

"A bit! Seriously, Van, you have been overdoing it."

Vanessa sighed in short acknowledgment. Jason had been in Europe for the last month, negotiating a deal with a Swedish company and setting up a branch of Carlysle Enterprises in London. In his absence, she had plunged herself into work, trying to fill the void left by the lack of his all-consuming presence. Contracts were pouring in now, and she was slowly getting used to the idea that Harrington, Inc., was going to have to take on a partner. She had been eating little and sleeping less, and the effects of this regime on her body were unfortunately all too visible.

The phone startled them both. "Who can possibly be calling at this time of night?" Vanessa stretched a long arm for the instrument.

"Dr. Harrington? This is Bill from Security. Sorry to bother you this late, but there's a little girl named Emily down here, says she has to see you. The cab driver who brought her needs to be paid, too."

He sounded worried, and Vanessa felt cold fingers clutch her throat. "I'll be right down." She was running for the door, grabbing her purse, calling a brief explanation to the alarmed Jilly.

The foyer was quiet at this late hour, and empty except for the white-faced, bedraggled figure of Emily Carlysle, the anxious Bill, and an equally alarmed cab driver.

"Emily, are you all right? Has anyone hurt you?" Vanessa dropped to her knees beside the child, hardly able to articulate the question as nightmarish possibilities flooded her mind and heart.

"Yes . . . no," Emily whispered, and burst into hysterical weeping.

"Dear God," Vanessa prayed, holding the child tightly to her.

"I didn't know whether to bring her here or take her to the police," the driver muttered, "but she seemed very definite."

"Shall I call the police, Dr. Harrington?" Bill asked.

Vanessa shook her head. "Let me try to get some sense out of her first. Emily, listen to me. I have to know—has anyone hurt you?"

The small head shook a vigorous negative and the three adults heaved sighs of relief. Vanessa fumbled with her purse, and paid the driver his fare with heartfelt expressions of gratitude. "I'll take her upstairs, Bill."

Back in the apartment, she and Jilly watched helplessly as the storm of weeping continued. There didn't seem anything to do except let Emily cry herself out, and at long last the sobs subsided into a series of breathless gulps.

"Now, Emily," Vanessa said quietly, holding the child on her knee, "tell me what happened."

Slowly, the whole sorry story came out. After a row of unusually momentous proportions with Diane that morning, Emily had decided not to go home after school. "I . . . I tried to call Daddy," she stammered, "but he wasn't there! He was supposed to be home yesterday. I wouldn't have run away if I'd known he wouldn't be there." A renewed attack of weeping accompanied the statement. "I called and called, Vanessa! I would have called Mama, only she was so angry this morning. And it got later and later, and I was so frightened . . ."

"Daddy will be there now," Vanessa said with grim conviction, imagining the horrified chaos that Emily's disappearance must have caused.

"But . . . but . . . maybe he's still in Stockholm."

"No, he was due in from Europe this afternoon; he had to change plans at the last minute," Vanessa explained firmly. "He had a meeting this evening in New York and was catching the last shuttle home." She glanced at her watch—it was after midnight. "He'll be home by now." Thoroughly exhausted, of course, she reflected grimly as she reached for the phone.

Jason answered on the first ring.

"I've got Emily," Vanessa said without preamble.

The long sigh at the other end of the line twisted her heart. "Is she—"

"She's not hurt, just exhausted and distraught," Vanessa interrupted the question, knowing the terror that lay behind it.

"I'll come get her," Jason said in a curious, dead tone.

"No, I'll bring her to you. You've done enough traveling for one day, and anyway, it'll be quicker. The sooner she's in bed the better."

She bundled Emily into the back of the Fiat and drove too fast through the relatively deserted city streets.

"Is Daddy mad?" the small voice whimpered in the dark.

"I don't know, sweetheart," she said frankly. "He's been very worried."

Jason was standing on the sidewalk outside the open front door as Vanessa pulled up beside the house. He moved at the speed of light to the car, wrenching open the back door. The white mask that seemed to have replaced his face gleamed for an instant under the streetlight and a voice that was not Jason's rasped, "This time, Emily Carlysle, you have gone *too* far!" The now wailing child was dragged bodily onto the sidewalk, propelled toward the house so fast her feet barely touched the ground.

"Oh, Lord!" Vanessa muttered, turning off the headlights with desperate haste, fumbling for her purse, locking the doors. Her one thought now to avert whatever was about to happen, she hurtled toward the house. Jason hadn't acknowledged her as he'd pulled Emily from the car, but the door was still open, whether intentionally or not she neither knew nor cared as she ran up the stairs to the living room.

"Jason, stop it!" She didn't pause to think of the consequences of interference this time. Nothing mattered but that she prevent Jason from doing something he would always regret and that his daughter would always remember. The child under his shaking hands whipped limply back and forth as if she were a rag doll, and with a strength she hadn't known she possessed, Vanessa tore Emily out of his hold.

"Keep out of this, Vanessa," Jason barked, a white shade around his tight mouth, a telltale muscle twitching in his drawn cheek. "This is between Emily and myself. It is *not* your concern."

"I am making it my concern." Vanessa spoke levelly, quietly, her hand holding the child's wrist with firm, reassuring pressure. She was making a stand and staking everything on that stand, but it didn't matter. She loved the father and the daughter, and she knew Jason and Emily must have nothing between them to regret. If Jason and Vanessa lost out—so be it.

"Move aside, Vanessa. I don't want to put you on the sidewalk, but I will, if I must."

Sharp pain knifed through her and the pulse in the frail wrist under her fingers began to race. She pushed the pain away.

"Jason, Emily's not a four-year-old who's just run across the road in front of a truck. She's behaved in a thoroughly reckless, inconsiderate fashion, but she *did* try to call you. Look, you've been scared witless," she continued rapidly, "but you can't take that fear out on the child. She *did* try to call you." She repeated the statement with desperate emphasis.

"Did you, Emily?" Jason was now struggling visibly for control and the child nodded dumbly, but Vanessa could feel the gradual relaxation in the small figure beside her, the slowing of the pulse. Emily knew her father, knew that he wouldn't behave irrationally once he understood.

"What time?"

"About five o'clock, the first time," Emily mumbled. "After I got to Dupont Circle. You said you'd be home this afternoon . . . but you weren't there!" The accusation hung in the air and Vanessa watched Jason take in the deathly pallor of the small, heart-shaped face, the eyes staring with shock, the tears pouring soundlessly, unrestrainedly down her cheeks.

Suddenly, he gave a deep, shuddering sigh and rubbed the heels of his palms into his eyes in a gesture of absolute fatigue that wrenched Vanessa's heartstrings.

"No, I wasn't, was I, poppet? Come here now. I think it's time you told me what caused this."

Vanessa let go of the fragile wrist and Emily ran toward the comfort and safety offered by those long, inviting arms. Jason sat down on the couch and took his daughter on his knees, cradling her head against his shoulder.

"Let's hear it, my love," he said quietly.

"Jakey was supposed to drive me to school this morning. Mama had a headache and didn't want to get up—she often doesn't," the child whispered. "But I didn't want to be late again—I've been late three times already this term, and after that I get Saturday morning detention—"

"Why didn't you tell me this before?" he interrupted.

"You told me not to tell tales," Emily wailed.

"All right, poppet." Jason's arms tightened around the child and Vanessa saw his knuckles whiten. "Finish the story."

"I got my breakfast and made my lunch," Emily continued tearfully, "and when Jakey didn't come downstairs, I went up to Mama's room. I said I had to go to school and Jakey said 'in a minute' and I said that I had to go now and Jakey said I was an im . . . an importunate brat, and I said he couldn't say that 'cause he wasn't my father and Mama got terribly angry and got dressed and took me to school."

So much intense emotion contained in such a continuous, rushed speech! Jason's face had gone even whiter and those gray eyes burned with an utterly frightening anger. With an abrupt movement, he stood Emily on her feet.

"I have to make some calls—half the D.C. police are out looking for you. I have to call your mother, too. She's out of her mind with worry."

"Come along, Emily. I'm going to put you in a hot bath," Vanessa said quietly, trying to control the sudden, violent shaking of her hands—the aftermath of that raw burst of emotion.

She led Emily upstairs, filled the tub, undressed the numb, small body, and lifted the child into the water. She was kneeling by the tub, gently washing the frail little figure, when Jason appeared in the doorway. He laid Emily's nightdress over the towel rack before wordlessly holding out his hand for the washcloth. Vanessa nodded, accepting the rightness of his move, and rose to her feet.

"I'm going to make you some hot chocolate, Emily." She left them together and went downstairs with her pain.

Jason's low voice reached her as she climbed the stairs to the child's room with the hot drink, and she paused at the open door. Emily was tucked tightly into the pretty canopied bed, with Jason stretched out beside her on top, holding her head in the crook of his arm. He was telling her a story—a ridiculous story about elves and rabbits and cottages on a hillside and his daughter, thumb in mouth, seemed to have regressed to infancy. That, Vanessa thought, was both right and proper and the most healing process in the circumstances.

"You forgot the bit about 'Tilda," Emily murmured sleepily. "When she gets away from the cat."

"So I did." Jason laughed softly. "I haven't told this

story for a very long time. Here's your drink, poppet. Sit up now."

Vanessa sat on the edge of the bed and listened as Jason continued the tale and Emily drank her hot chocolate. When she reached to take the empty mug and rose to her feet, the child seized her skirt.

"Please stay, Vanessa," she pleaded suddenly, her gray eyes becoming overlarge in the little face.

Vanessa hesitated, and then Jason's firm voice broke the quiet. "She's not going anywhere, poppet. We'll both be downstairs if you need us." He got off the bed, kissed the little girl with just the right degree of brisk reassurance that signaled an end to the whole business including an end to babying, and waited by the door as Vanessa also kissed Emily. With a small sigh, the child curled into a tight ball and closed her eyes.

"You've lost a lot of weight, firefly." Jason spoke suddenly as they reached the third-floor hallway.

She flushed and bit her lip. Her heart was beating uncomfortably fast and for some reason she couldn't seem to catch her breath.

"An ounce or two, maybe." She turned toward the guest room.

"Where are you going?" He caught her arm, and for a moment they stood sculpted in silent immobility, Vanessa still facing the far door, Jason holding her arm gently but firmly.

"It's very late," she said quietly. "I'm going to bed in the guest room."

"The only bed you're going to be sleeping in, Vanessa, is mine." It was a flat statement in the tone of voice Emily would have recognized as brooking no argument.

Vanessa sighed. She didn't feel strong enough to deal with anything right now. Too much had happened in the last couple of hours; too much had been said, and even more left unsaid to drag heavily on her weary soul. She'd fought and won a battle for Emily and Jason, but her right to fight that battle had not been acknowledged—indeed, quite the opposite. Jason had actually threatened to put her out of the house if she interfered in what he saw as a totally private affair—his business, nothing to do with her at all. Her shoulders slumped with deathly fatigue. If it hadn't been for her implicit promise to Emily, she would have walked quietly out of the house, driven to the sanctuary of home and Jilly's unfailing sanity.

"Jason, I think it's best if I sleep in the guest room tonight. I'll stay just until Emily wakes up in the morning."

"I think perhaps you didn't hear me." He spoke softly, still not releasing her but making no attempt to draw her close.

"I heard you."

"Then get undressed and into bed. I'm going to make us some tea." He let her go then, walking steadily down the stairs to the kitchen.

She watched that broad, retreating back for a moment before marching resolutely to the guest room. Undressing quickly, she went into the adjoining bathroom. It was well equipped, right down to the new toothbrush in the holder. Typical Jason! His eye for domestic detail was infallible. She scrubbed her teeth with a vigor bordering on violence, then returned to the guest room and crept between the crisp sheets of the bed. She heard footsteps on the stairs, the clink of china, and for an instant tensed, then relaxed. Jason was far too civilized a person not to recognize and accept the tacit statement made by her refusal to share his bed.

But the door opened, the overhead light snapped on. Instinctively, Vanessa covered her dazzled eyes with a bare forearm.

"Lost your sense of direction, firefly?" the rich voice inquired smoothly. "You're in the wrong bed, my sweet."

The covers were stripped from her body, and for a moment she lay, eyes covered, stunned into immobility.

Jason's voice suddenly broke the instant of quiet. "What on earth have you been doing to yourself, Vanessa? You're skin and bone!"

An embarrassed shyness filled her, to be chased away almost immediately by anger. How dare he calmly strip her and then comment in that critical, exasperated tone on what he saw? Hastily, she sat up, grabbing for the covers.

"Get out of here, Jason. I'm fulfilling a promise to Emily, but, so help me, I'll break that promise if you don't leave me alone. I can't talk right now!"

"Whatever you've been doing, it clearly has to stop." He ignored her statement totally, scooping her off the bed into his arms.

Vanessa wrestled with herself for the barest instant. She was too well accustomed to Jason's habit of simply picking her up and putting her where he wanted her to waste precious energy in futile struggles.

His own room was softly lit, drapes drawn across the long windows, Chopin dancing gently through the elaborate stereo system set into the hessian-covered walls. Jason held her against one upraised knee as he pulled back the covers on the enormous bed, inserting her gently between the silky, dark-blue sheets, pulling up the pillows behind her head, manipulating her body into comfort.

"You can't be cold, firefly, but you've certainly got the shivers," he remarked matter-of-factly, pulling the sheet tightly across her breasts, tucking it firmly under the mattress. "I think you need a little Chivas Regal in your tea."

He was totally impossible! Vanessa lay back against the pillows, filled with helpless frustration. He'd put Emily to bed and now he was calmly doing the same to her.

"Jason, I don't think you understand." She spoke to his broad back, watching as he poured tea into two delicately fluted white porcelain cups, reflecting quite irrelevantly that this very large man surrounded himself with only the daintiest, most elegant possessions. His furniture stood on the delicate carved legs of antique craftsmanship, his china and glass shimmered and gleamed with the finest bone and crystal. Emily appeared to treat these possessions casually, but Vanessa had never once seen Jason blanch as the child clattered dishes and glasses, and she had never seen Emily break anything, either.

"Oh, but I do understand, my love—at long last." Jason spiked the tea with a generous slurp from the dark bottle before turning to her. "Drink this and let me tell you what I understand."

Sitting on the edge of the bed beside her, he held out one cup, and with a sense of total helplessness she took it, inhaling deeply of the fragrance before sipping, shuddering slightly with pleasure as the hot soothing liquid burned its fiery way down her throat to curl comfortingly in her stomach.

"You've just saved me from making probably the biggest mistake of my life." Jason spoke slowly, his large hands curled incongruously around the delicate cup, his eyes fixed at some point in the middle distance. He turned toward her suddenly. "Oh, put that damn cup down, firefly! I can't say this to you unless I'm holding you."

She complied silently and he pulled her out from the tight, confining sheet, settling her on his lap. "Not cold?" he asked anxiously, wrapping his arms around her.

She shook her head, waiting quietly for him to continue.

"I can't believe I said what I did," he whispered painfully. "I didn't mean it, little love. It was just a reflex action—I've spent so many years dealing with things alone that I just forgot, for one dreadful moment, that I have you now. I think I've only just understood how much I need you. I needed you tonight; Emily needed you—your strength, your wisdom, your love. And you gave them to us both, in spite of my rejection. Oh, my love, can you ever forgive me? Can you ever trust me again?"

The voice carried none of its usual strength, only a soft, almost desperate plea, and Vanessa slowly raised her arms to encircle his head, to pull him down against her breast as she ran long, stroking fingers through his hair.

"I love you," she affirmed quietly. "I need you, too, and I could never imagine a time when I couldn't trust you to be there for me, just as I'll always be there for you."

Jason gave a deep, shuddering sigh, then raised his head slowly. Their lips met in the gentle promise of total faith and commitment.

After a long, long time his face left hers. The old gleam returned to his eyes as he said sternly, "I want an explanation from you."

"Oh?" Her own eyes laughed up at him.

"Why have you become so incredibly skeletal?"

"I'm *not* skeletal!" She struggled to sit upright but gave up as his hold tightened. The muscular thighs beneath her tautened, supporting her naked, wriggling body.

"You *are* skeletal, my sweet. Thin may be in, but there are bones here that should *not* be visible!"

Vanessa, subsiding against his chest, grimaced. "Jilly calls it burning the candle at both ends."

"Well, if you value a whole skin, little love, you'll ensure I never find you burning that candle at either end!"

She chuckled. "Playing macho man again?"

"I'm not immune to temptation." He grinned. "Hop back under the covers while I pour us some more tea. I have to tell you what I've been doing." He put her back in the bed with competent efficiency, refilled their cups, and resumed his seat on the bed. Then, abruptly, he asked, "Could you take Emily out of town for a few days? To Hatteras, maybe?"

"I'll need to reorganize things, but yes, I could," Vanessa said thoughtfully. "Why?"

"I'm about to spill the beans." His lips curved in a travesty of a grin. "Ever since that awful birthday lunch, I've been working with an army of lawyers to find the most bloodless method of getting sole custody of Emily."

"But why didn't you tell me?" Vanessa exclaimed. "You were evasive when I asked you if you were doing something, and if I didn't ask you, you never said anything!"

"I know. I have a habit of keeping my problems and their resolutions to myself," he agreed sadly.

"*Had* a habit," Vanessa warned him.

"Yes—*had*." A feathery fingertip touched the end of her nose fleetingly. "Anyway, I think I can now convince Diane, particularly after today, that if I went to court I'd win. There are certain aspects of her life-style that just might not appeal to a judge." His lips tightened bleakly. "I'm prepared to give her a fairly hefty settlement and the usual visiting rights."

"Buy her off, you mean?" She stared in shocked amazement.

"Nasty, isn't it?" he said evenly.

"Will she agree?"

"Oh, I should think so." A short, bitter laugh accompanied the statement. "But Emily's going to have to get used to eating more hamburger than lobster if her mother pushes as hard as I'm sure she will."

"I don't exactly earn peanuts, you know?" Vanessa protested roundly.

Jason stretched a long hand, pulling the sheet away from her. His flat palm rested on her stomach, bringing tiny prickles to life across the entire surface of her skin.

"I was hoping you might agree to take a leave of absence once or twice. A few more Carlysles won't make that much difference to this complicated business."

"Are you asking me to marry you, Mr. Carlysle?" Vanessa struggled for a severe formality, although laughter bubbled in her chest and her body was beginning to dance under the sensuous stroking of his practiced hand.

"Good God! Did I forget? What an appalling omission!" Jason dropped on one knee beside the bed, features schooled to an appropriate gravity.

"Vanessa Harrington, would you do me the honor of giving me your hand in marriage?"

"So long as you don't expect obedience." Her eyes sparked mischief.

"Whose? Yours or mine?" he growled, rising to his feet with one fluid movement, then dropping down beside her on the bed.

"Neither," she whispered as his clothed legs pincered hers and she reached for the buttons on his shirt.

"Male or female Carlysles?" She reverted to the original subject as her hands ran slowly, luxuriously, over that well-loved body.

"We'll leave that to the gods and the genes; but right now I'd like to get a little practice."

"Seems logical." She slipped down the bed, offering herself on the altar of those loving hands.

Epilogue

"DEFINITELY LESS PROVOCATIVE!" The low, sensual murmur, the unmistakable feeling of her bikini sliding slowly off her hips, brought Vanessa startlingly awake as she lay facedown on the back deck of the Hatteras house.

She made an instinctive movement to turn over, but something in the small of her back pressed her down. "Jason, is that you?"

"And just who else were you expecting?" he inquired severely.

She grinned and gave herself up to the wonderful sensation of the hot May sun and his hands roaming over her back. "How long have you been here?" It was an effort to speak as honeyed warmth spread through her languid body.

"About half an hour. You were sleeping like the dead. I was going to leave you for a while, but the thought crossed my mind that you'd look much less provocative naked than with this ridiculous piece of string around you. I'm afraid the temptation to prove my hypothesis became irresistible." His voice rippled with amusement as his hands continued to work their wizardry and her body shifted deliciously under his touch.

"I think, perhaps, we'll take them right off," he went on matter-of-factly, and the thin strip of material was drawn down her legs and over her feet. At the same moment, the pressure on her back lifted and she rolled slowly over, now completely naked, to regard the laughing face above her through eyes narrowed against the glare of the noon sun.

"Mmmm. Still a bit scrawny," he teased, "but not quite so drawn and tired."

"Bastard," she commented without rancor, sitting up on the thick beach towel, drawing her knees up to her chin, hugging them against her.

Jason laughed softly, turning toward the picnic table, pulling a napkin-wrapped bottle out of an ice bucket. He was barefoot, wearing only a pair of denim shorts, and her eyes roved greedily down the powerful, muscled back, the strong, well-shaped legs.

"You have a beautiful body," she observed casually, resting her chin on her knees. "What's that?"

Jason turned the label of the bottle toward her, his eyes alight with merriment.

"Wow!" she breathed. "Now I really am puzzled."

"Why so, firefly?" His hands were busy with the wire around the cork.

"Well, if you won your fight with Diane, I can't imagine how you can afford Dom Pérignon. And if you lost it, why are we celebrating?"

Jason chuckled and walked across the deck to stand over her. "The battle, my sweet, is won. I am, indeed, a poorer man today than I was yesterday, but it's going to be a very rainy Monday when the budget won't run to an occasional bottle of Dom Pérignon!"

"I'm relieved," she murmured. "I'm only marrying you for your money, after all."

His eyes gleamed appreciatively. "Lie down, witch. I have a fantasy that I want to enact."

Now what? Vanessa thought with a soft smile of antic- ipation as she lay back. Life with Jason Carlysle would never be boring, that was for sure. "Ow! Jason, that's cold!" She jerked as the icy, bright drops filled her sun-warmed navel.

"Keep still, for heaven's sake," he instructed. "You'll spill it!"

"You're quite absurd, Jason Carlysle," she declared

roundly, trying to lie still and control the gales of laughter that threatened to upset the unusual cup. Jason's dark head bent and his velvet tongue began to lap the wine from her body. Her eyes closed in involuntary pleasure as he licked the last drops from her skin.

"Well," he remarked suddenly, lifting his head. "In the fantasy, the champagne didn't taste of suntan lotion, and there weren't little bits of gritty sand, either!"

Hilarity swooped through her and she curled, gasping, on her side. "Do I get any of that?" she demanded, once the storm had subsided somewhat.

Jason was still kneeling beside her. "You want it in a glass, or have you a more imaginative suggestion?" He grinned.

"A glass will do fine—I'll leave the imagination up to you!"

He poured the golden bubbles into two shallow glasses. "My imagination is working overtime right now." He dropped down beside her again, eyes glowing with desire. "But since I have no wish to be disturbed while I exercise it, what have you done with my daughter?"

Vanessa sipped her champagne, regarding him thoughtfully over the rim of her glass. "You're not going to believe this."

"I'll believe anything where that child is concerned." He sighed. "Did you drop her off the end of the pier?"

Vanessa chuckled. "Don't be absurd. She's been utterly angelic."

His eyebrows disappeared into his scalp. "Angelic! Come on, firefly—that's going a bit too far!"

"Noah has taken her fishing," she declared.

"You've got to be kidding!"

"Not so!" Her head shook vigorously. "Your daughter has totally captivated that misogynist so-and-so, and I can tell you I am getting *very* fed up with 'Noah this and Noah that.' They won't be back till sundown."

"Thank God for Noah!" He took the empty glass from her hand.

"Oh, I forgot to mention," she murmured innocently, as

he pushed her backward on the deck. "Gideon and Melissa are arriving later this afternoon."

"To hell with Gideon and Melissa, whoever she may be! By the time I've finished with you, Vanessa Harrington, soon to be Carlysle, you are not going to be able to stand on those pretty feet!" His tongue plundered her ear, his teeth nipping the tender lobe as her hands stripped him of his shorts.

The ocean crashed, sending sand crabs scuttling, and the hot sun stroked their undulating bodies as the fragrance of sun-warmed wood mingled with the scent of their love.

"Jason?"

"My love?"

"I love you."

"And I love you, my own, with every breath I breathe."

The world disappeared, toppling slowly around them as infinity beckoned.

WATCH FOR 6 NEW TITLES EVERY MONTH!

Second Chance at Love ®

All of the above titles are $1.95 per copy except where noted

All of the above titles are $1.95
Prices may be slightly higher in Canada.

HERE'S WHAT READERS
ARE SAYING ABOUT

Second Chance at Love ®

"I think your books are great. I love to read them as does my family."
— *P. S., Milford, MA**

"Your books are some of the best romances I've read."
— *M. B., Zeeland, MI**

"SECOND CHANCE AT LOVE is my favorite line of romance novels."
— *L. B., Springfield, VA**

"I think SECOND CHANCE AT LOVE books are terrific. I married my 'Second Chance' over 15 years ago. I truly believe love is lovelier the second time around!"
— *P. P., Houston, TX**

"I enjoy your books tremendously."
— *I. S., Bayonne, NJ**

"I love your books and read them all the time. Keep them coming—they're just great."
— *G. L., Brookfield, CT**

"SECOND CHANCE AT LOVE books are definitely the best!"
— *D. P., Wabash, IN**

*Name and address available upon request